Miklowitz, Gloria D.
Close to the edge

Close to the Edge

Also by Gloria D. Miklowitz

Close to the Edge

GLORIA D. MIKLOWITZ

DELACORTE PRESS/NEW YORK

Published by
Delacorte Press
1 Dag Hammarskjold Plaza
New York, N.Y. 10017

For Lester, Irene, Joyce, and Spencer
and for Jeanette Sobel Schmelzer,
who gave me my first book.

My special thanks to Bebe Willoughby, my editor, for her
careful readings and valuable suggestions, and
to Beverly Horowitz for her input and encouragement.

Manufactured in the United States of America

First printing

Library of Congress Cataloging in Publication Data
Miklowitz, Gloria D.
Close to the edge.
Summary: In spite of having all the advantages money
can provide, high school senior Jenny sees little point
in life until she volunteers to play the piano for a
senior citizens' band and receives the benefit of
elderly wisdom.
[1. Conduct of life—Fiction.   2. Family life—
Fiction.]   I. Title.
PZ7.M593Cl   1983   [Fic]   82-72817
ISBN 0-440-00990-1

1

I can't remember when I'd felt so empty and hopeless. Standing at the bedroom window of the ski
condo at three in the morning, and shivering in my
flannel nightgown, I didn't even care. Behind the
curtain the frosted window felt icy to my touch,
and beyond that was the snow, banked up to within
a foot of the top of the glass.

I thought of Poe's story about the man bricked
into a tomb, and the captor's terror and hunger to
live. I knew exactly how he felt.

From upstairs I heard Dad's deep snore and the
sound of the refrigerator cycling. In the bed next to
mine my younger sister Amy slept, so still she might
be dead. In the room next door were my brother
Eric, and Bret, his college roommate, home for the
holidays.

If only I could sleep. Almost every night of our
Christmas vacation I'd awakened after a few hours
with the same gnawing ache of loss, a sadness so
heavy it felt like rocks in my chest. I'd lie in bed or
stand at the window and try to figure out why I
hated myself. Hated my life. Found everything so
pointless that even my music gave me no joy anymore.

Everyone thought I had it all—good health,
good looks, brains. I had friends, even a special

boyfriend. I lived in a nice home with the same parents who gave me birth, which in itself was remarkable considering the times and our social standing. Nothing money could buy was denied me, at least not for long. I even drove my own car.

"Jenny?"

I turned to see Amy propped up on one elbow in bed, rosy and sleepy-eyed.

"What are you doing?"

"Nothing. Just thinking. Go back to sleep."

Amy yawned and stretched, then shivered.

"You cold?" I asked. "I'll get another blanket."

"No. Just scared."

"Why?" I sat on my bed and pulled the bedspread around me.

Amy slithered back under the covers but propped the pillow up behind her head so she could see me better. "I promised Eric I'd ski Dave's Run today. I promised, and now I don't want to."

"But you've only skied from the top a few times this week. You're not experienced enough. It's tricky."

"I know."

We gazed at each other, not speaking. I felt sick, disappointed. My older brother, a heartbreaker, judging from the stories he'd told all that week, cared first and only for himself. To him, it was a kick to bait Amy. But was I so different? Wasn't my whole family that—thoughtless, uncaring?

"He says it's not as hard as it looks, that he'll even go down first, show me the way."

I went to her bed and sat on the edge. "You

don't have to, Amy. Nobody can make you. Just say no."

Amy bit her lip thoughtfully. "He'll say I'm chicken."

"So?"

"I don't want Eric to think I'm chicken."

"Sticks and stones and all that..."

She nibbled the edge of her thumb, then asked, "When did you first ski Dave's Run?"

I lifted a strand of hair from her mouth. "Not till I was fourteen, two years ago."

"Oh!" She brightened. That meant she had three years to go. "Well, maybe I'll wait then. Next year, maybe."

"Sure. Now get some sleep."

She yawned again and turned over. "Night, Jen, and thanks. See you tomorrow."

I went back to bed and climbed in. My hands and feet felt icy now. Tomorrow was here already. And it would be no better than today.

"Okay, you guys! If you're not ready in one minute, you stay behind!" Dad had just come in from starting the van and loading the skis. I could hear him stamping his boots. "Amy? Rick? Jenny? On the double!"

I zipped up my yellow parka, pulled the thick wool ski cap with its silly pompon over my head, and went out to gather the ski poles in the dark corner of the downstairs entry. Mom, in a green velour bathrobe, leaned over the upstairs banister.

"You're not coming?" I asked, looking up at

Mom. That choked-up, tearful sound was in my voice again.

"Nope. Last night's party was a bit much. Besides, someone's got to get us packed to leave." She bent forward, searching my face. "You okay?"

I smiled and tossed my head and with some effort put life into my voice. "Sure, what else?"

"Keep an eye on your sister, will you, Jen? I heard Eric talking up Dave's Run to her, making it sound like a bunny slope. She might be crazy enough to try it just to win his approval. You know how she is."

"Sure, Mom, sure."

Mom's leaning over the balcony and watching made me want to fly up the stairs and into her arms. But ours wasn't that kind of family. We didn't hug or kiss much and Mom never saw me as needing such shows of affection. Nobody did. Jenny was the self-confident, self-sufficient teenager who had it made. Slightly cynical, but together. That was the image I put out at school. That's how my friends saw me. I'd gotten away with it for so long that nobody even noticed that I wasn't alive inside. Maybe the whole world lived like that. Two selves. The public one and the private one.

"Be back by four, Liz," Dad called up finally. "Let's be on the road by five!"

Mom saluted, a wry smile on her lips. "*Oui, mon général!*"

"No joking, Liz!" He talked as though Mom were one of us kids.

"Absolutely! Well, guys, have fun!" Her look returned to me briefly but it seemed as if she'd already forgotten what she might have sensed. I glanced away.

We stopped to pick up Dad's partner, Dr. Williams, and his family, plus two others, so we were ten in the van on the drive to the mountain. All through the vacation it had been that way. The group. People visiting back and forth, in our condo or theirs. Parties. Crowds at the lifts, on the top of the mountain. You were never alone, except for those few minutes on the slopes coming down. And at night, when everybody was asleep.

It was easy to sit back, pretending I wasn't quite awake yet, because everyone talked at once.

"Amy's coming up with us today, gonna try Dave's Run," Eric said, bringing me out of my half-sleep. "Aren't you, cookie?"·

I'd been leaning my head against the wall of the van, eyes closed, but listening. I opened my eyes now to see Amy wide-eyed and tense, watching Eric.

"Amy's a natural. No fear at all. Good judgment, fast reactions, gonna be better than any of us."

"Yeah," Bret said. "I saw her take the gondola run. Smooth. Just took off like there wasn't a thirteen-hundred-foot drop."

"I, uh," Amy tried, then threw me a scared cry-for-help look.

Eric put his hand on her shoulder and grinned. "I saw an eight-year-old kid up there yesterday. If he can do it, so can you."

"She's not skiing Dave's Run," I said quietly.

Eric threw up his hands in terror. "Help! The mummy's come to life!"

I glared at him and didn't answer.

"Amy can think for herself, sister dear."

"Then let her. Don't set it up so she can't say no, like telling her any little eight-year-old can do it."

"Amy?"

Amy fiddled with the loose fingers of her glove and didn't answer.

"No big deal, Rick. Amy and I are getting off at the halfway station together. Maybe later we'll go to the top."

"Amy?"

She looked up, begging Eric's forgiveness, and nodded.

"How come, cookie? I never figured you'd be chicken."

"Maybe next year," she murmured.

Eric shrugged. For the rest of the drive he talked with Bret and the others. As long as Amy didn't do what he wanted, she didn't count.

From below, Mammoth Mountain seemed an enormous, wide iceberg, flecked with brightly colored dots zigzagging down its steep slopes. Chair lifts swung skiers high up over the snowy pines and rocks to the dozen or more runs down its front face. We would take the gondola, which climbed first to a midway station, then went on up to the top.

Standing in line waiting for the gondola, I didn't

feel part of it all. My nostrils burned from the cold and dryness. Around me skiers talked and joked, stamped their feet, and hugged themselves to keep warm. Bret tugged playfully at the long hair hanging below my cap and put an arm around my waist. I gave him a smile and pulled away. Just leave me alone, I thought. Especially—don't touch.

Amy and I got off the gondola at the midway station. She looked back regretfully at Eric, hoping for a word. "Have fun," Bret called after us, but Eric only waved. And then we sloshed through the dirty, melted snow inside the building to a bench outside to put on our skis.

"You can go now, Jen. I'll be okay," Amy said. "I know you'd rather ski from the top. Really. I don't want to ruin your day. Besides, I saw a friend already."

I patted her head, then impulsively gave her a quick hug. "See you later, then, Amy." Quickly I unlocked my skis, crunched back over the snow into the building, and grabbed the next gondola going up.

Once the gondola left the midstation it climbed even more steeply, gliding upward almost without sound except for the eerie howling wind outside. I shivered. I'm never in a gondola without a feeling of uneasiness. It's as if I'm not quite part of the living—in limbo.

We sat, six strangers, making small talk or looking out. Below, skiers flying downhill; behind, the miniature toylike buildings of the inn and lift station. On my right, the Minarets, jagged-peaked and grand, marched across the horizon against a bleak gray sky. Ritter and Banner, the tallest peaks, were mostly hidden by dark, heavy clouds promising more snow. I felt myself part of the stark, brutal landscape, and my throat ached with unshed tears.

Moments later we reached the top. The gondola paused briefly, then jerked into the dimly lit station, slid a short way, swung clumsily about, and stopped. An attendant steadied the swaying bubble and unlocked the door.

Outside, skis and poles in hand, I looked back as the empty gondola started its return down the mountain. What was I doing here? I thought in surprise. Where was I going?

I clamped into my skis, changed sunglasses for goggles, and tugged my cap tighter over my ears. Resolutely, I pushed off. Signs pointed the way to the various runs. Already my gondola companions were disappearing in those directions. I hesitated. For a moment I thought about the choices. Huevos? They said it was steep, a chute between rocks, and I'd never dared. Philippe's Col? The sharpest drop of them all, Eric boasted.

Without much conscious thought I changed direction, cross-countrying steadily away from the gondola station and the approved slopes on the face of the mountain.

"Hello! You there in the yellow jacket! Return to the building, please!"

I stopped and looked back. A ranger holding a megaphone stood on the gondola-station balcony motioning to me. "Come back, miss!" he called again. "That area is closed to skiers."

I turned around. He watched me for perhaps twenty-five feet, then went back into the station. For a second I hesitated, then reversed direction.

Suddenly I knew what I would do, where I would go. The knowing brought a rush of panic and tears, fogging my goggles. *No! It's crazy*, part of me warned. *You can't. Sssh*, another part chided. *It's nothing. It's not so hard. And anyway, it doesn't matter one way or the other.*

I pushed my way across the snow against the wind, crying and scared, but with a kind of wild elation such as I hadn't felt in months. Soon, looking back, I couldn't see the gondola building. It seemed as though I were the only one left in a big, white-swirling world.

I stood at the edge shuddering, looking down. The unmarked slope with its unknown obstacles dropped steeply, but no more so than other slopes I'd skied. To the left, near the bottom, trees.

From the back of my mind I pulled forth a memory. Down that rocky slope, through those trees, to the left was the *Hole-in-the-Wall*. The *bottomless pit*. "Like a volcano with a drain at the bottom," someone once explained, "flowing out to an almost vertical drop." *A treacherous ride. Risky even for the most expert skier*, which I was not.

I was so tired. So many nights without sleep. So many days watching the world from behind a mask of pretending. So tired. With fluttering fingers I adjusted my goggles and repositioned the ski poles.

Eyes closed, knees bent, every nerve, muscle, and cell in my body tensed. Standing firm, with the wind at my back, I imagined how it would be. The push-off. The first yards of control, of concentration and exhilaration. The gathering speed, the moments of hysteria as speed turned to recklessness. That awful moment just before hurtling down the devil's volcano to the tiny hole at its base. Rocketing through—to . . .

My heart thudded so hard it seemed it might burst. Tears blurred my vision. The wind nudged me and it took fierce control to hold firm.

— Go! the inner voice whispered. Go!

I screamed into the wild, swirling whiteness.

And pushed back.

2

January third. Two days later. And now it's back home and life as usual. School.

"Hey, Jenny!"

"Hi, Allison."

"How was Mammoth?"

"Fabulous. How was Aspen?"

"Fan-tas-tic! Met this gorgeous . . ."

"Gee, Allison. Love to hear, but gotta go. Call you."

I threaded my way through the crowds of kids decorating the wide high school steps. Every afternoon from sixth period on, the steps become a social gathering place, especially for juniors and seniors. Kids lounge against the pillars or sit on the steps catching up on who's going with whom and who said what and where next weekend's party's going to be. It's hard getting past friends without stopping, especially after a long holiday with so much to talk about.

But I smiled, nodded, returned the hi's, and kept picking my way between bodies to the street. Today, somehow, all I wanted was to get home. As fast as possible and before Amy or Mom so I could slip into my room and just be alone.

Down the street toward the parking lot I saw April and the gang on Hillcrest's big rolling lawn. April, smoking as usual, seemed pale and worn, as if she hadn't slept much recently, a sign her parents were away again. Everyone figures her dad's worth millions, but April dresses as though she buys her clothes on bargain days at the Salvation Army Thrift Store.

Michelle slouched next to April, trying to be four inches shorter than her five foot eleven. She looked great, tanned from her week in Palm Springs and wearing a new sundress which looked as though it had cost a bundle. It usually did. When her father got the bill it would almost surely bring in return a pleading phone call reminding her he had two families to support now, to have pity. But any call, even an appeal for mercy, was better than none at all.

Susan, as usual, seemed to be hanging on April's every word. She was new to our group and seemed to think every dumb thing we did was wonderful.

If April hadn't waved, gesturing for me to join them, I'd have pretended I hadn't seen them, but now I had no choice.

"Hey, where ya been all day? When'd ya get back?" April asked. "How was old Mammoth?"

"Lots of snow. Lots of family togetherness. Lots of partying."

"Any guys?" Susan asked, eyes wide with interest.

"The usual." I turned to Michelle. "What's new?"

"What do you mean by the usual?" Susan persisted.

"She means *the usual*," April said, blowing a

noseful of smoke into the circle so that I coughed and Michelle waved the air with exaggerated motions. "Doctors vacation in packs, like wolves, you know. That way they don't have to talk with their families. They bring their wives along, of course. First, second, or whatever. Their progeny, too. Which brings us to the guys. More wolves, like their daddies. Right, Jen?"

"You got it." I wished they'd drop the subject. And then April said, very offhand, "You hear about Cindy Bickford?" She dropped her cigarette in the grass and slowly, deliberately, ground it in.

"Yeah!" Susan echoed, an unusual level of excitement on her face.

"What about her?"

"Nothing. Except she tried to snuff herself, is all."

"She what?"

"OD'd, or tried to. Her mother found her."

"Cindy? But she wasn't into drugs!" My tone sounded shrill and accusing even to me and I started to shake.

How would I know what Cindy was into these days? We'd been friends through sixth grade when I'd lived on her block, trading Nancy Drew books and whispering together about sex and problems at home. She used to be so sad when her father left on a trip. He traveled a lot for a computer company. Her mom loved to sew and by the time we moved to upper Hillcrest had started an alterations business in her home.

Mom had some dresses shortened there and I'd

go with her to see Cindy. But after a while she said it was just too much trouble taking me there just to visit.

For a while Cindy and I still talked by phone and saw each other at school. But gradually I fell in with Michelle and April. Lately we just kind of nodded when we passed.

The girls were falling all over each other telling what they knew. I listened, but felt more and more sick as they talked. Why Cindy? I was sure she wasn't a loadie. At our school few kids were into drugs as much as alcohol lately. Was it because she didn't fit into any particular group? She wasn't a nerd, a kid who studied a lot. And for sure she wasn't a sosh, though I suppose she wanted to be. I suddenly remembered the last time I'd talked to her about a month ago.

We met by chance in the school rest room and tried to make small talk. Somehow we got on the subject of college and she said, "It's easy for you. You're smart and talented. You could be anything you want to be."

"Me?" I'd pointed at myself in surprise because I'd never thought about myself in that way. For a moment I dropped the pseudo-noncaring air I usually wear for social contact. "I wish I *knew what I wanted to do*. Really want to do," I admitted wistfully.

"Now, me," Cindy had said, "I'm just average. Average looks, average brains, average everything. I can just see my listing in the yearbook. 'Cindy Bickford Average Nobody.' "

I was embarrassed. "Hey, don't put yourself down so much. You're a nice person. Lots nicer than some I could name!"

Cindy had blushed and then gazed up at me with a kind of hopeful expression. It wasn't hard to guess what she wanted. For a second I thought about inviting her to join our lunch bunch, then didn't. We wouldn't have much in common anymore. The group was big enough. Instead, I averted my eyes, shrugged, said something empty like "tah tah," and left as fast as I could.

"But why?" Michelle was asking. "Why would she do such a thing?"

"Maybe she was pregnant."

"Don't be an idiot!" I blurted. All Susan ever thought about was boys and sex. Yet, was it possible? My mind scanned all the times I'd seen Cindy and it had never been with a boy. Besides, what girl today doesn't know about birth control? And even if she were pregnant, would she kill herself because of it? I bit my lip. "Damn!"

"Let's not get morbid. She's okay. She'll probably be back at school tomorrow." April pulled a new cigarette from her purse and dangled it from her lips.

"Hey, did you guys hear about Laura?" Michelle asked. "Know who she's seeing?"

Michelle went off on a long story describing how she'd heard the news and what she thought about it while I, still quivering with the news about Cindy, felt a million miles away. Without even saying good-bye I turned and started to the parking lot.

"Hey, Jenny! Where you going?" I heard behind me.

"Home," I called back. "See you tomorrow." Then I picked up my pace until I was running.

I'd been given the red Porsche convertible on my sixteenth birthday in October. To celebrate we'd all gone to dinner at the country club. The Hillcrest CC isn't exactly my idea of a fun place. It's mostly stuffy old-money people and the rooms are rich with dark woods and velvets and a noise level never above a whisper. But the food is good, the best in Hillcrest.

I'd noticed the car as soon as we got out of our Mercedes for valet parking. It was parked between a Cadillac and a Rolls, which made it look especially little and sleek and almost alive with its fire-red finish and white leather interior.

"Wow, will you look at that!" I said in awe. "Now, there's a car I'd sell my soul for."

"I wonder whose it is," Amy said, giggling unexpectedly.

"It is kind of nice, isn't it. Racy. Rather like it's slumming amongst these . . . these . . . uh . . ." Mom gestured with a well-manicured hand and left the sentence unfinished. As he so often does, Dad finished for her. "Like these overfed boors?"

"Yes."

For a moment we all stood there admiring it, then Dad got us moving into the restaurant and the car was forgotten.

After dinner two solemn and elderly waiters

came to the table with a candlelit cake. I groaned. Waiters singing birthday greetings are so square. I suffered through the ditty with a false smile, then cut the cake. At last Dad presented me with this small box.

"To my beautiful, bright, lovely daughter," he said, eyes sparkling.

"Our," Mom corrected softly. "Our daughter."

"Of course." Dad kissed me. "Happy birthday, sugar."

I thought by its size the box had to contain jewelry, a ring or bracelet, maybe. I pulled off the satin ribbon and unwrapped the gold paper, then lifted the lid. "Well, and what have we here?" I asked dramatically.

Amy threw conspiratorial glances at my parents and Mom looked younger and happier than she had in a long time. Within the folds of tissue paper I felt around but couldn't find anything resembling an object of any kind. Aside from the card with its greeting, the box seemed empty.

"Underneath! Look underneath!" Amy cried, tongue stuck out and body thrust so close it was clear she wanted to find it for me.

At last I found it, taped to the bottom of the box. A key. I held it up, attached to its chromium ring. It was small and gold with numbers on it, but nothing more. "It looks like—a car key?"

Dad nodded.

"A car?!"

"Well, not just a car, a rather special one," Mom said.

"What's red and white and parked outside?" Amy asked breathlessly.

"You didn't!" I clapped my hand over my mouth. Voices carry far in that big echo chamber of a dining room. "The Porsche?" I whispered, looking from Mom to Dad. "I don't believe it!" I grinned my delight across the table. "Oh, Mom, Dad, thanks! You can't imagine what this means! I'll love it forever! I can't wait to drive it!"

"Go ahead." Dad shook his head and smiled.

I jumped up, kissed each of my parents, even my sister, then ran across the restaurant nearly catching my dress on a chair, and losing the flower pinned in my hair.

The Porsche had been the most exciting, most wanted gift in my life. I couldn't have asked for anything better.

So how come, I wondered now as I climbed into the driver's seat and slung my day pack in the back —how come the thrill had been so short? Here it was January. I'd had the car for a little more than two months. It still looked new, even smelled new. I'd only put a little more than a thousand miles on it. Guys still whistled at it. Older drivers still pulled up beside me at red lights, honked, and asked how "she runs" and what kind of mileage "she gets."

Plugging the key into the ignition now I felt irritable, wondering how come owning the car didn't do a thing for me anymore. "Because," a little voice crowed, "all it is is a car. A fancy car. So what. What's the big thing."

"Hey, Jenny!"

I recognized Brian's voice even before glancing back over my shoulder. Brian and I had been dating about two months. We'd met because of the Porsche, as a matter of fact. Two months was supposed to be a record for him according to the school grapevine, so I was looked on with a certain amount of envy and respect by girls who wished they were in my place. I felt pretty good about it; at least I had at first. But now I know Brian pretty well, and it's not all that great.

"When'd you get back? I phoned last night, about nine. Nobody answered," he shouted. Half of his six-foot-three-inch body stuck out of the sunroof of his orange VW and he was grinning. The best thing about Brian is that smile. Maybe that's what makes him such a good entrepreneur. He could sell heating systems on the Equator and people would buy. He'd sold me on doing more things than I really wanted to do, so I should know.

"Got home late, after eleven. The traffic was fierce," I shouted back. "Why? What's up?"

"Tell you later. Going home?"

"Yeah."

"Race ya."

"Brian, no!"

He'd been trying to get me to race him for a month now, insisting his VW could outclass any sports car, including my Porsche. I said it was dumb using the streets of Hillcrest as an Indy 500 course just to prove that his car or mine was the faster, or that one of us drove better.

"Aw, come on, Jen! Just once!"

"Oh, okay!" I said wearily. "*Okay*. Then maybe you'll stop bugging me."

"You win and I'll be your slave for a day. I win, you go to the prom with me in May. How's that for sweetening the deal?" He watched me, smiling coyly.

I should have been thrilled. Instead I got a sinking feeling. He'd gotten his way again. He usually did.

Did I really care about Brian? About going to the prom with him? Not really. He was such a rotten listener most of the time. Sometimes I got so bored with all his talk about making money. And for all our intimacy, I didn't often feel close to him. Then I thought, Stop it! There you go again, discounting everything: car, boyfriend, everything. Maybe you expect too much.

"Fair enough?" he repeated, stretching his arms wide so his plaid Ralph Lauren shirt pulled tight against his broad chest.

"Why not." I'll invite him in when we get home, I thought with a surge of hope. I'll tell him about Mammoth, about how it seemed those ten days, about all the things I saw and sensed. Maybe this time he'll listen. And if he does, then I'll tell him the rest. For one quick second the Hole-in-the-Wall flashed through my head and sweat poured down my arms.

I put on the large-framed sunglasses I always keep in the glove compartment. Then slowly, with my eyes on the rearview mirror, I backed out of the parking space and pulled parallel to Brian's VW. Brian, behind the wheel, smiled at me across the space between us, revving his engine. I nodded, leaned back against the white leather seat, and gripped the wheel with both hands.

"Better wait till we clear the parking lot," I called over the din of both engines. "See you on the road." I took off with a spurt of speed, easing the gears from first to second and third. Taking the lead, I hogged the double space, not letting the VW pull alongside until we were well out of the lot and into the road. Okay. He'd gotten his way; we'd race. Okay, then I was going to win. I waited till Brian pulled parallel.

"Ready?" I'd fly those 3.2 miles home in under three minutes, even with the light at Cambridge Street. I'd show him how good a female could handle a car, how great my Porsche was, even if it was a *she*.

"Say when!"

"*Now!*"

I pressed my foot on the accelerator, one hand on the gear shift, eyes intent on the road ahead. My Porsche shot forward, past kids in clusters, past parked cars, past palm trees and neatly clipped broad lawns and expensive-looking homes. A cool breeze, smelling of the ocean and orange blossoms, blew my hair about my face. The sun felt good. I was aware, always, of the orange VW, sometimes almost edging past me, sometimes running alongside, with Brian screaming something until a car came toward us, forcing him back. But not me. Never me. I clutched the wheel in a fierce grip and smiled. Come on, death, come on. I dare you.

A block from Cambridge I could already see the blinking red caution light and accelerated to sixty-five, determined to cross the intersection before the light changed. Brian, behind me, would have to stop.

But halfway down the street I saw the woman. She had just stepped off the curb, a child on either side. Fear tingled in my wrists, spurted up my arms and down my legs until my whole body shook. Oh, God! I thought, braking and pressing the horn at the same time. In the quick glimpse I managed the woman seemed surprised, then scared. The Porsche skidded and swung left, then I became so busy trying to keep control, trying to keep it from climbing up the opposite curb, that in the next moments I lost sight of the woman and only felt a hot swoosh of air as Brian shot by with a shout of triumph.

I think I screamed.

When I finally gained control and returned to my lane I had crossed the intersection through the red light, barely missing a car. Ahead, Brian was disappearing in a blur of orange. My heart was hammering. My palms were wet. My lip was bleeding and I felt like throwing up. Through the rear-view mirror I searched for the woman and children. A car on the cross street blocked my view at first. Then I saw them. The woman bent over the two children gathered at her skirt. Their small bodies pressed against her. They were alive.

Trembling and eyes blurred with tears, I pulled to the curb and cut my engine. Then I laid my head on my arms over the steering wheel and just sat there waiting for the shaking to stop. We could have killed them, I thought. I could have killed myself! What was I trying to do? Is that what I wanted?

When I pulled into our driveway a few minutes later Brian was waiting at the curb. He was leaning against his car, arms crossed as if he'd been there an hour. And smiling. "What took you so long?" he called.

I parked the car, climbed out, and reached into the backseat for my pack without so much as nodding his way. Then I marched down the path to the front door. With trembling fingers I put the key in the lock and turned. Brian appeared immediately by my side.

"Hey, what's wrong? You mad or something?"

I gave him a look which said how I felt.

"Look, if it's because of that dame with the kids . . ."

I opened the door and started to go in.

"Hey, I didn't even scratch them! I'm a damn good driver. You know that!"

"We could have killed them."

"Oh, hell. It was just a little harmless fun!"

"It was dumb. Dumb. Stupid. Mean!"

"Aren't you going to ask me in?" Brian leaned

against the doorframe in that casual, sexy pose he sometimes strikes. Usually, when he looks that way, I go soft inside. But this time, seeing him in those designer jeans and shirt and sixty-dollar Adidases, I just felt disgusted.

"Brian, go home." I tried to close the door. How had I been so dense. Only minutes ago I'd fantasized about asking him in. Sharing my deepest fears with him. Dumb. Brian didn't have the capacity to understand.

Brian looked puzzled and hurt. "Well, if that's the way you want it. But I thought, since we haven't seen each other for nearly two weeks, we could talk."

Talk, the magic button. One hand on the door and swallowing tears, I hesitated. All right, maybe I was being too sensitive. Give him another chance. "Do you mean that?"

"Of course. I've got a lot to tell you."

Hopeless. All he wants is to talk about himself. Without any particular expression, almost holding my breath, I asked, "Did you hear about Cindy Bickford?"

"Cindy? Yeah. Tough. Worked on my campaign once. Nice kid."

I nodded, waiting for more.

"You going to ask me in?" He flashed his boyish, playful grin and toyed with a strand of my hair. "Hey, been two weeks . . ."

What more did I expect Brian to say about Cindy? I don't know. "Brian, go home. Please? I'm just not feeling too well, okay?"

He looked doubtful and backed away from the doorway slowly, watching me, still hoping. "If that's what you want." It seemed an hour before he was on the sidewalk near his car. All that time I faced him with a forced smile, pretending everything would be fine, that there was nothing wrong between us that couldn't be fixed.

I closed the door at last and stood against it for a long time listening to the sounds of the house, to the air rushing through the heating system vents, to Amy's hamster exercising on his wheel in the family room, to the grandfather clock's steady heartbeat in the living room.

And I thought about Cindy Bickford.

3

Cindy Bickford, Jenny Hartley. What was our connection? Why did I feel so awful at the news of her suicide attempt? Was it only because I'd drawn back when I sensed her need for friendship?

Was it because she'd touched me in a way my other friends never had—seen something in me I'd not even recognized myself? Or was the connection her despair and how she'd tried to deal with it?

I shuddered in the warm entry hall and refused to follow that thread further. What was wrong with me? I bitched at Brian, but I was just as guilty as he. I didn't have to race him. I didn't have to take the lead, baiting him to pass me, knowing his ego couldn't stand losing. How come nearly everything drove me to tears lately?

It's a mood; it will pass, I decided. Do something. Keep busy. Don't think.

But I couldn't get Cindy out of my mind. Maybe I should call her, see if I might visit. Yet what would I say?

I dropped down on my bed and lay on my stomach, hands supporting my head. What was Cindy's room like these days, I wondered as I looked around my own. Did she live in a page out of *Architectural Digest*, too? Bed with white organdy canopy and spread. Yellow-and-white furniture.

Cleaned twice weekly by a hired genie who came and went without ever being seen.

Before I could think too long and change my mind, I reached for the phone directory in the nightstand. There were a dozen Bickfords, but only one on Arden Road. I picked up the receiver and dialed.

As soon as the phone started ringing, I got a scared, fluttery feeling inside. It had been nearly five years since I'd phoned Cindy. What would I say?

"Hello?"

"Hello. Mrs. Bickford? This is Jenny Hartley. Is Cindy in, please?"

Pause. Silence. Did Cindy's mother remember me?

"She isn't able to come to the phone just now. She's . . . ill."

"Ill? Oh," I said. "Will she be coming back to school soon?"

Pause, almost electrified. "We hope so."

"Can she see visitors? Friends?"

"I don't think so. Maybe in a few days. We'll see."

I felt subdued, almost relieved. "I'll call back in a few days, then, Mrs. Bickford. And please tell Cindy I phoned. Jenny Hartley."

"I know. Thank you, dear. I'm sure she'll be pleased."

I hung up and stared at the phone, still tied to it as though to an umbilical cord. Cindy was at home. How would she feel knowing I'd called? How full of pretense and dishonesty we all were, I thought. Cindy's *ill* for all who call, but everyone knows what really happened. *I'm* Cindy's friend; some friend!

Despite my thoughts, the call made me feel better. I wandered down to the kitchen, where I finished off a yogurt and took an apple from the basket on the counter. It felt good being alone in the quiet house. What had happened at Mammoth seemed a bad dream and I'd not dwell on it. For the first time in a long while I thought of music. Shining the apple on the side of my skirt I walked into the living room. Late afternoon light slanted through the wood-shuttered windows, leaving a pattern on the rich dark walnut of the Steinway.

I took a deep bite out of the apple and placed it on some sheet music. Then I sat down on the bench, opened the lid, ran my fingers up and down the keyboard, and for the next hour I played.

"Not again!" It was Mom's voice coming from the kitchen. "Didn't you see enough of those men these last two weeks?"

"I can do without your sarcasm," Dad said sarcastically. Then his voice dropped too low for me to understand.

"Why didn't you marry *them*? They see more of you than I do!"

"There you go again. Making mountains of molehills. We were together constantly for the past ten days."

"Together? Is that what it's called? You better

get a dictionary and see what the word means!"

"Liz!"

"No! This time you'll hear me. I don't know you anymore. You slip in and out of the house and we don't talk. You surround yourself with people, like you're afraid to be alone with me. You think you spent ten minutes with our kids during the whole vacation? I mean *ten minutes* alone, talking, and listening! Tell me, did you?"

"Mom, don't," I whispered. "Don't. Please don't." I put my hands over my ears.

"Keep your voice down!" Dad commanded. Then, in a whisper, something about "opening a can of worms."

Mother's voice dropped. I recognized the tone. She would be shivering with intensity because she hardly ever stood up to Dad. "What do you know about your children?" she said in a quavery tone. "Know what Eric is majoring in at Dartmouth? You think premed? Think again. Girls! Have you any notion of what's going on in Amy's life, what a spoiled brat that little one is becoming because you never back me up—because you can't say *no*?" Mom paused just a second, then she almost whispered, "Do you know anything about that older daughter of ours, the one who wears armor?"

My head seemed to be vibrating. My legs, too. And my whole body burst out in a sweat.

"Dinner ready yet, Jen?"

"What?"

Amy, doing an around-the-world with her Duncan yo-yo, came into the dining room. "Why are you covering your ears? Got an earache?" she asked.

I pulled my hands away and tried to focus on my sister. She watched me closely while running the yo-yo up and down. Amy is tall and well developed for an eleven-year-old, as I was at her age. She's olive skinned and dark haired, like Mom, with a sultry, pouty look that Dad says will "wow" the guys someday. I didn't want her to hear the ugly goings-on in the kitchen. "Dinner's not ready yet," I said, turning her around. "Let's go up to my room. You can try on my new lip gloss."

Later the four of us gathered around the dining table. Everything was in its place. But tonight everything felt wrong, out of tune. We weren't at all what we appeared to be. Maybe we never had been. Even though it wasn't the first time Mom and Dad had quarreled, I wondered now what kept them together.

"Well," Dad said, taking his napkin from its ring and smiling first at me, then at Amy. "And what have my princesses been up to? Amy? What's new at school? Any problems?"

Mom delicately picked at the cold poached salmon, rearranging the food, not eating. *He's trying, Mom*, I thought, sending out thought waves. *Give him a chance. He's trying.*

Amy told a long story about a trip the sixth grade planned to the Sierras next month for survival training. I listened, watched, felt oddly removed. It was a trip I'd taken years ago. We'd learned to build snow shelters and make fires, and to identify edible berries and roots. Later I recalled thinking that most of us enjoyed it for the chance to skip a couple of days of school and be with friends. What, after all, did Hillcrest kids need survival training for unless it was for surviving their parents' divorces?

Dad listened attentively to Amy, showing Mom how wrong she was. Now and then he asked a question, nodded, and not once did his eyes leave Amy.

"It only costs a hundred fifty dollars. But I do have to buy a down sleeping bag, too, because we'll be sleeping in cabins with just wood-burning stoves."

"Only a hundred fifty dollars, Amy?" Mother asked the question with a kind of innocent amazement.

"Yes, and I can get a neat down bag at the Sport Chalet for only a hundred twenty-five!"

"*Only* a hundred twenty-five. How nice. Will you ever have use for that bag again, Amy?"

My sister didn't understand. She looked from Mom to Dad. Dad saw where Mom was leading. Oh, Mom, I thought. He tried, and you spoiled it!

"Who do you expect will pay for this trip, Amy, the hundred fifty dollars plus the hundred twenty-five dollars, plus spending money for three days in the snow? Will it come from money you saved from allowances?"

Amy opened her mouth, closed it, and looked beseechingly at Dad. Everyone knew Amy couldn't hold on to money.

"Come on, Liz," Dad chided. "Don't take it out on her. After our little stay in Mammoth, what's another three hundred bucks?"

"It's not just the money." Mom leaned forward, body rigid. "It's the attitude. Our daughters had better marry rich men, because they have no concept of how to earn or save."

"Like mother, like daughter, hey?" Daddy caught my eye and winked. "Anyway, we've got it, so why not spend it?"

"Right, why not." Mother shook her head in defeat. "That's why we've failed them. They've always had too much, too soon. And it's as much my fault as yours. And that's all I'm going to say on the subject."

A smile froze on Dad's lips. "Phew!" He pretended to wipe the sweat from his brow. "To think all this started so innocently, just over my going out to play a little backgammon with the guys tonight."

Dad and Mom locked eyes, and they were like two enemies, shield against shield. Mom looked away first. Then Dad shook his head, wiped his mouth with a napkin, and rose from the table. He tossed the napkin down and nodded to Amy and me. "You can reach me through my answering service if there's an emergency." With that, he stalked out of the dining room to the kitchen, and from there to the garage through the back door.

The three of us sat there not saying a word, listening. The car door slammed and the engine started up. Mom's hand shook as she lifted a glass of water to her lips. She seemed to shudder as the car spun out of the garage and down the drive to the street.

I concentrated on buttering a French roll, breaking it in half and smearing the butter in as deep as I could. Then I couldn't seem to eat it.

"Does that mean I can't go on the survival trip?" Amy's voice trembled.

I threw her a look to shut up, and Mom didn't answer.

For the rest of the meal everything tasted like rocks. Was this what life would be fifteen or twenty years down the line?

Sometimes it's better not to think too much, especially about parents. After all, what can you do about them? If they hate each other, they divorce, like Michelle's folks. They don't bother asking their kids if they'd mind, because it's their business, not the kids'. So I figured whatever would be with them would be. I had my problems; they had theirs.

And in the morning Mom and Dad seemed okay again. True, they were super polite. "Pass the cream, please," and that sort of thing. Dad even gave Mom a polite kiss on the forehead and winked. Mammoth never happened. And last night never did either. When you don't think about the past, it disappears.

The way to hold on, I figured, was to play it easy. Mom's right. Dad's right. Don't take sides. And better I should let it all roll off me. That way it wouldn't hurt.

That's the attitude I took when I went into the

counseling office the next day for my annual "checkup" with Mrs. Schwartz. Once a year we go over things. "How are the grades? What are you up to? Any questions? Bam, bam, good-bye." That sort of thing. You can almost write Schwartz's dialogue before you go in, and it usually doesn't vary much from the way you imagined it.

"Oh, yes, Jenny Hartley." Schwartz looked up from the file and smiled. "Sit down."

I sat.

"Well, and what are you up to these days?"

"Not much."

"Let's see. You're a junior now?"

"Right."

"Going to college, I suppose? Sent for your applications yet?"

Most of the kids at Hillcrest go to college. It's a parental sentence, whether or not you've got the makings. Yes, I'd sent for applications, at least some.

"Where do you want to go?"

I told her. They were some of the better private colleges in the state. Dad had narrowed the field down.

"Well, let's see how you stack up." She shuffled the papers again. "Your GPA's fine. Keep it up and you're in good shape gradewise." She smiled at me over her half-glasses. "Take the SATs yet?"

"In October."

"Oh? Yes. *Very* good."

When I'd gotten my SAT scores I'd figured they'd mixed me up with someone else.

"Now, how about teacher recommendations. Oh, yes, a few. Not great, but good."

I said nothing. When I'd asked my poli-sci teacher for a recommendation he'd given me a five-minute lecture first. "You're too cynical for such a young person, Jenny. Instead of standing around and condemning the world, why don't you get in there and do something about it? Get involved." I'd made some off-the-wall remark about maybe running for Congress someday and he'd sighed and taken the sheet I was holding out. He'd be too chicken to say what he really thought on the recommendation. Hillcrest teachers wouldn't dare; their contracts wouldn't get renewed.

Schwartz took off her half-glasses and waved them back and forth. "You know, Jenny, the top schools can afford to be choosy. They get hundreds of applicants with as good grades and even better teacher recs than you have. What it comes down to when they're making the final decisions is how well rounded the student is. They don't want just grinds. They want good students with curiosity, and social conscience, and interests beyond school."

"You mean interests other than boys, skiing, and race cars," I said, pretending innocence.

She shook her head as though she couldn't imagine why she bothered with the likes of me. "Did you join any clubs? Work on the school paper? Get into sports? Take part in any of our volunteer placements?" Her frown looked pained. She knew the answer.

"I never had time."

"Others did."

I could just hear April on that subject. "Why should I kill myself on some dumb swim team or waste my time writing about chess club meetings for the *Log* when I could be home listening to records or out with my friends?" In my nearly three years at Hillcrest, I'd joined nothing. While some volunteer programs sounded interesting, the kids I hung around with just didn't go for it. We called it "busy work." For peons.

"Guess I've blown it," I said lightly. "So I don't get into my choice of school. There's always junior college." I stood up.

"Sit down," Schwartz barked. "And don't give me that 'I couldn't care less' attitude. You care if you get into a good school, and so do your parents. So let's see what we can do."

"What can 'we' possibly do? Maybe 'we' should invent a good record."

"I'll ignore that, Jenny, because I know you don't mean it. It's a shame you didn't think about this when I mentioned it last year. But that's water under the bridge."

"How about the radio station placement?" I asked. Three hours volunteering there might not be so bad. "That would look nice on the applications."

Schwartz ignored me. She was running a finger down a list, stopping now and again, then moving on. "We have two seniors working at the radio station now."

"Hospital volunteer? My dad's a doctor, so I know something. And while I don't have a lot of respect for the medical profession, I wouldn't mind."

"Filled, with a long waiting list." Schwartz continued to scan the sheet. "You know, Jenny, you might think of this in a positive way. Helping others is a two-way street."

"Think not what your country can do for you, but what you can do for your country." As soon as I'd said it, I felt bad. It's strange how often what I said came out the opposite of what I felt. "Sorry."

"You play an instrument?"

"Piano and flute. Why?"

"We've had a request for someone to accompany a musical group for two hours a week."

"Oh? What kind of group?"

"A kitchen band."

"A *what*?"

"Washboards, pots, kazoos, that kind of thing."

"That's music?"

"They're a group of elderly people. The Sunshine Seniors. Their pianist broke a hip and they haven't been able to find a replacement. Some of them were fine musicians at one time, but now they play for fun." She seemed to be measuring me, trying to judge how I felt.

"Sunshine Seniors, what an icky name."

"Ever been around old people, Jen?" Schwartz asked. "Are your grandparents around?"

"Only one grandmother. My mother's parents are dead. Grandma lives back East. Actually, I hardly ever see her." Fleetingly, my mind called up Grandma Horowitz. Though our last name is Hartley, it used to be Horowitz. Dad changed it years ago, before I was born. Later he changed religions, too. What I remember of Dad's mother isn't terribly clear. An apartment in New York with dark, heavy, old furniture, lots of pictures and knickknacks, a smell of cooking.

Grandma stood only as high as Mom's shoulder and scurried about like a windup toy getting us tea, putting out platters of cookies, exclaiming over Amy and me and telling Eric in a funny accent how much he resembled Dad at that age. She pulled out photographs and albums and tried to keep us longer. Daddy seemed comfortable, but I remember Mom smiling a lot and talking in that fast, high-pitched voice she uses when she's ill at ease. Now and then she'd glance at her watch.

When it was time to go, tears came to Grandma's eyes. She hugged me good-bye, feeling bony and breakable and smelling of a very sweet cologne. "Write to me, dear. Tell me all about your friends and what you're doing. Will you promise?" I nodded. But I never wrote.

"I think you'll like this placement, Jenny. Here's the number to call to set up the time and place." Mrs. Schwartz noted something in my file, then handed me a slip of paper. Beside a phone number was the name Solomon Katz.

"And remember," she added. "If you expect to include this service on your college applications I'll expect you to stay with it through June. No excuses."

"Yeah, promise." The cynical side of me was

already figuring how the gang would react. They'd ride me plenty about joining the enemy, the "doers." They'd think it hilarious that I'd be with old people, old people who played toy instruments, yet. For sure they'd want the details to make good jokes.

Well, so what. Maybe keeping busy with something new was exactly what I needed. Some people, I'd noticed, kept so busy they didn't have time to think. Maybe that was the secret of life, to getting from day to day. Just—busy-ness.

4

Brian had called me the night before to apologize. I don't think he really knew what it was he was apologizing for, only that he'd better or he'd likely not see me again.

"Accepted," I said wearily after I'd heard three different versions of the same "sorry." There didn't seem to be much purpose in breaking off with him. What he'd done really wasn't much worse than what most of my friends would do. I mean, what about my treatment of Cindy?

I forgot he'd be waiting outside Schwartz's office. He'd caught me at my locker in the morning and we'd arranged to meet after my appointment. He sprang off the bench near the door and loped toward me, smiling uncertainly. "Everything okay? Schwartz throw you any curves?"

The "everything okay" was asking about more than the meeting with Schwartz. No use making him suffer. We'd go on as before because he wanted to and because, in superficial ways, we went well together. For the things that really mattered to me like music, honesty, and such—well—I'd have to find someone else to share them with.

"Would you believe I'm going to be accompanist for a senior citizen band?" I assumed the slightly cynical style of talk Brian seemed to like from me.

"No kidding? Jenny Hartley and the Over-the-Hill Gang! How about that!"

" 'Service is good for the soul,' Schwartz says." I rolled my eyes skyward. "And for college applications."

"Oh!" Brian said.

"Where we going?"

"Thought we'd go someplace and talk. You wanted to talk, didn't you?"

Yes. Yesterday. Before the car race. Before his reaction to Cindy. Now there wasn't a chance in a million I'd tell him about Mammoth. "Sure. Let's go to the beach."

"Oh. Thought we might go someplace more private. Your house, or mine."

Brian's parents both worked. His dad's a lawyer and his mom's a translator. Unless it was the cleaning lady's day, we'd have the house to ourselves. The same at my home. Tuesdays Mom took a class in Cuisinart cooking and didn't come in until five and Amy went to a friend's house after school. No. If we went to either house it wouldn't be to talk. And though we hadn't been together in two weeks, I didn't feel loving enough to want that now. "The beach will be beautiful today," I said with a smile.

He didn't look pleased, but he didn't object. "Then it's the beach. I'll drive."

"Like yesterday?"

"No, promise. Yesterday really was dumb, like you said." He flashed me that winning smile and held up two fingers in a scout salute. "Honest. I'll hold it under eighty."

"I'll drive."

"Okay, fifty." He deliberately bumped me in the hip and laughed. "Wow, it's great to see you again!"

As far as he was concerned, we were back to normal.

On the drive to the beach Brian chattered on about the holidays. He hadn't left the city as we did because both his parents were tied up. "Besides, I needed the time to work out some plans. Like, remember that rock group I booked for the Halloween dance?" He glanced my way for a second. "The Rip Offs?"

I nodded. Sometime, way back in sophomore year, Brian had taken on the job of finding talent for special school events. Mimes, singers, jazz and rock combos on their way up, or down—depending on how you looked at it because some of the talent was pretty awful.

"Well," he said, both hands on the steering wheel and grinning at the road ahead, "I'm going to represent them! They dumped their agent and asked me to take over, said they liked my style."

"But they weren't very good, were they? I mean, seems I remember we all kidded about how their name was well chosen, considering."

"No sweat. It's all in the packaging. Dress them up in a style everyone will remember, give them a shtick, see they have one good repertoire, and I'll get them into every high school within a hundred miles. And that's just the beginning!"

Just like Brian. It's not the talent, it's the packaging. The flash. Just for a buck. "Well," I said with false admiration. "Today Hillcrest, tomorrow the world, right Napoleon? Or was it Caesar? Or maybe Hitler?"

I'd gone too far and didn't care.

Brian took it as a compliment. He laughed and put an arm around my shoulder.

We pulled into the beach parking lot and took a blanket from the trunk, then, shedding our shoes, headed out to the sand. It was warm from the January sun and empty for miles, except for occasional lovers on blankets, sun worshipers, and joggers along the surf punching holes out of the wet sand as they ran. We spread our blanket and walked to the breakers, hand in hand.

"So," Brian said. "Tell me about Mammoth. Did you miss me? I missed you a lot. I must have thought of you a hundred times. Nearly took off to see you just before New Year's, but my car broke down. I'm sure glad you're back!" He pulled me closer, arm around my waist.

Before vacation I'd really thought I liked Brian, maybe even loved him. But once away, I hardly thought of him. Hadn't missed him. Not one day. What was it like, loving someone? Did it make you happy to be alive, glad about each day? What a marvelous feeling that must be. I wished Brian made me feel that way.

I told him about the holiday. About the skiing and the weather, the new restaurants and who was there we both knew. I said nothing about the early mornings or of what had almost happened. Not a word about the way the future looked to me.

My tongue danced along as though it had a life of its own, making Brian smile or laugh. But all the while Mammoth intruded in little glimpses and feelings. All of a sudden I'd think about standing at that edge, looking down, all the awful imaginings of what it would have been like if I had pushed off.

"Hey, what's wrong?" Brian asked when I started to shiver. I tore myself free and began running. A wave crashed against my legs and I cut my foot on something sharp, but it felt good. It reminded me I was at the beach, and safe.

"Cindy didn't get the drugs from Monty and his crowd," Brian said sometime later. His words came to me through a haze of babble about other things. Brian loved to talk and I'm a good listener.

We had climbed out on the jetty until we reached a big, flat rock at the end. Around us the ocean surged and ebbed. Huge waves crashed against the rocks, showering us with spray. Brian stood, legs wide apart, throwing shells far out into the surf while I sat facing out to sea, arms around my knees, just staring. Until he spoke about Cindy, I'd been far away and nowhere, only half listening.

"What? What did you say?" I shouted above the noise of the surf.

"Cindy didn't get the drugs from Monty and his crowd."

I stood up, brushed off some sand, and nearly lost balance as a wave broke against the rocks.

"I did some checking," Brian shouted, offering a hand. "It seemed strange, her OD'ing. Didn't figure her for a loadie."

He tossed a shell far out into the water and we watched it cut through the dark surface and disappear. "Seems she went to this party and everyone was high. Smoked some pot, had a few drinks, then went home. No one thinks she got it from them. They say no one was dealing, so she couldn't have bought anything that would do her in."

"Then where? And why?"

Brian shrugged and looked for more shells. "Who knows."

For a few minutes neither of us spoke, then I asked, "Brian? Have you ever thought about it? I mean, have you ever felt so lonely, so sad, like life really had no point and what difference would it really make?"

"Thought about it, sure. Everybody does at some time or another. But do it? Never. My God. I've got so many things to look forward to, so many things I want to do."

Brian looked at me. "How about you?"

I shook my head. "Thanks, Brian, for asking around, for trying to find out about her. Thanks." I reached up and kissed him, tasting salt on his lips.

He hugged me close, burying his face in my hair. Then he took my hand and we started the tricky return over the wet, mossy rocks of the breakwater, to the beach.

When I reached home Mom was in the kitchen playing with her new Cuisinart, a gift from Dad at Christmas. I stopped in the doorway, kind of looking for a chance to talk. You'd think, with a mother who doesn't work and a father who keeps office hours only five days a week, that would be easy. It's not. These last few years we move around the same house and tell each other what's for dinner and where we've been or are going to, but that's about it.

"Hi," I greeted, almost shyly.

"This machine is fantastic," Mom announced, her back to me. "Just look at that!" She flipped a switch on the Cuisinart and the machine whirred and the stuff in the glass jar on top began twisting and turning like a big hunk of Silly Putty. "Look at how it kneads bread dough! I can make all kinds of breads from now on!"

Marvelous, I thought. Dad has his Betamax for TV programs he misses the nights he's out, and his Apple II computer for fun and games, and now Mom has her Cuisinart. Machines, the love substitute.

"Mom, turn it off and talk to me."

She threw me a surprised look but turned off the machine. It became very quiet in the kitchen. "Okay, it's off. What do you want to talk about?" She started removing the dough from the processor.

"Can't that wait?" I sat down at the breakfast table and hid my hands in my lap.

Mom left the Cuisinart, took some cups from the

cabinet, and poured coffee for us both. Then she came to the table. "What's up?"

For a few seconds I traced the pattern on my cup, wondering where to begin. Then, without looking up I said, "A girl at school tried to OD."

"That's terrible!" Mom exclaimed. "Do you know her?"

I hesitated, then looked Mom straight in the eye. "It was Cindy. Cindy Bickford."

Mom's eyes opened wide. She said, "Cindy! Is she all right?"

"I think so."

"Why? Why would she do such a terrible thing!"

"I don't know. Maybe she was very depressed."

"Lots of people get depressed, especially in adolescence, but they don't commit suicide!"

"Maybe she couldn't find any reason."

"Reason for what?"

"You know, to go on living."

Mom gave me a long look. "Do you ever feel like that?"

"Sometimes."

"Well." She smiled. "It's the age, the hormones, that's all. When I was your age I was up one minute and down the next. When I was really unhappy I'd sometimes picture myself at my own funeral. Everyone would be crying, sorry they'd been mean to me." She laughed and shook her head. "But I never once really meant it seriously!"

"What's so great about life, anyway?"

"Jenny, come on, now. Think of the alternative!"

I shrugged.

Mom put a hand on my arm. "You're young and lovely and have everything in life to look forward to. Think of people with some horrible illness. They'd give anything to be in your place."

"I know." I sipped my coffee and didn't look at her.

"Then, cheer up! And stay away from her. It's too depressing. You have so many *nice* friends."

"Mom!"

"I mean it! And keep busy. When you keep busy you don't have time to think all those silly thoughts about life and its meaning and all that."

When we'd started talking I'd hoped it would be possible to tell Mom what had happened that last day at Mammoth. Now I knew I couldn't.

"Jenny?" Mom lifted my chin and made me look straight into her eyes. "Don't let me hear you talk like that again. You have nothing to be depressed about. Understand? Now, smile."

I couldn't.

"I'm sorry about Cindy, but that's *her* mother's problem, not mine. Not yours, either."

I drank my coffee so she couldn't see my lips tremble. Mom smiled encouragingly as if the subject was closed and whatever she'd said had made everything all right. Then she turned around to look at the Cuisinart. Soon after that she got busy putting the bread dough in loaf pans and talked about some of the people in her class. As soon as I could, I left the kitchen and went to my room.

Mom had meant well, I suppose, but she didn't

understand. But maybe her advice to keep busy made sense. I'd pretty much come to that conclusion myself. Okay, I'd do that. First, homework. Then, phone calls to friends. Maybe later I'd play the piano again.

Which reminded me of Schwartz and the Sunshine Seniors. I went to my purse for the paper with Solomon Katz's name and phone number. "Go ahead," I said to myself. "Phone him. It's part of the therapy. Old people must know something, to have lived so long." I picked up the phone wondering what the man at the other end of the line would sound like. Then I punched the buttons and waited.

Solomon Katz's first words to me when I told who I was and why I was calling were "So, speak a little louder, darling. A person, he gets to be eighty-six, he don't hear too good."

"My name is Jennifer, Jenny Hartley," I repeated louder, enunciating each word carefully. "From Hillcrest High. You called Mrs. Schwartz? You need a pianist for your band?" Weird. If he couldn't hear me, how could he conduct a band?

"So! Wonderful, Jenny Hartley. You read a little music, maybe?"

"I should. I've taken lessons for nearly seven years."

"A regular Paderewski!" he said, chuckling. "You don't mind playing with a bunch of old fogies when you should maybe be out playing with nice boys?"

I hesitated, not knowing how to answer the question, but Mr. Katz just chuckled again. "Never mind, Jenny. I like to make jokes. So tell me, darling. Hartley. What kind of name is that? You're not Jewish?"

"Well, uh, no. Not exactly. Why? Does it make a difference?" I cleared my throat. What a strange question to ask.

"Of course not. Whatever you are, it doesn't matter. It's only good you want to help. It's nice, young people, when they remember the old."

I didn't answer, wondering what he would think if he knew the real reason behind my volunteering. "Is there any music you want me to bring, Mr. Katz?"

"No, darling, thank you. Sadie left it all in the piano bench. But there is one thing you could help."

"Sure, Mr. Katz. What?"

"Me, I don't hear too good. You noticed? So, like a good girl maybe you would make some calls? Since Sadie broke her hip it's three weeks we haven't played. You could phone the members, maybe, tell them we're in business again?"

"Sure, Mr. Katz. Just give me the names and numbers."

It took another twenty minutes before I'd written down the eleven names and phone numbers of the band members. First, Solomon Katz had to find his reading glasses, which took a long time because even his distance vision "wasn't like it used to be" when he was a young man of seventy. And then he had to read from the list, adding side comments about this one who might be visiting her daughter, and that one who just got out of the hospital, and that one who maybe gave up her phone because she couldn't afford it with the cost of living going up so high every day. But at last I had it all down, including alternate numbers and where we would meet, the date and time.

"So, darling," Mr. Katz warned before hanging up. "Now I have something to tell you. You drive careful. Go slow. You get there five minutes late, it don't matter. You're alive. Understand?"

"Yes, Mr. Katz. I'll be careful," I said.

"And Jenny. The neighborhood. It's not so good anymore. Hoodlums. Crazies with the drugs. Muggers. You should look around when you come; be careful."

"Yes, Mr. Katz. I will." I shook my head and looked up at the ceiling. My goodness! Eighty-six years old and he's still worrying about staying alive! By that age you'd think he should be sick of it all, wanting out.

Yet he was kind of dear and funny, caring like that. I hung up the phone and sat thinking. And then I found myself grinning. That devil! What a snow job he'd pulled. How come he wasn't making the calls? He'd heard me on the phone just fine, despite his complaints. And look how he'd conned me into another hour or two of work on the phone *because he couldn't hear.*

5

Dad's not usually at breakfast because he leaves early to make hospital calls, but the next morning there he sat reading the paper, coffee cup in hand. "Who was on the phone all evening?" he asked, looking up. "I tried calling home a dozen times and each time got a busy signal."

"I was. Talking to some senior citizens who have a band. I'm going to be their accompanist. It's a volunteer thing for school," I said pouring myself some juice and looking over the dry cereal choice. "I'm sorry, but they talk a lot. Give them half a chance and they tell you their life stories."

Dad nodded. Then he went back to reading the business section.

"Old people. Yuck!" Amy made a face over the rim of her milk glass.

"What's yuck about old people?" Mom asked. "Someday your dad and I will be old."

"You'll never get old," Amy said. "You'll never get like that, all wrinkled and stretched and saggy, with skin that hangs to here." She held her left hand a foot below her right upper arm.

"Beauty is only skin deep," Dad announced without looking up.

"Amy's doesn't even go that deep," I said.

"You're obese," Amy said. "And I bet you don't even know what that means."

"Girls, enough. Eat your breakfast and get off to school. You'll be late." Mom brought a plate to Dad with two sunny-side up eggs and toast. "Talking about old people, you really should give some thought to your mother," she told Dad. "It's not good for her living alone, so far from us. And the neighborhood has deteriorated terribly. Did you notice last time? She had three locks on the door. She's virtually a prisoner."

"I know," Dad said irritably, snapping the paper into a long fold. "But you heard what she said. 'You can't uproot an old tree and plant it someplace else and expect it to live.' And she won't even consider an old age home."

"Yes, but . . ."

"Do you want to bring her here? She keeps the thermostat at eighty-five, winter and summer. You told me yourself you couldn't stand it. You could hardly wait to get out of there."

"Now, just a minute!" Mom said. She had returned to the stove for more coffee and was standing with her back to us, hands on the counter. She turned around. "You're laying the blame on me and that's not fair. I'm always the bad guy, just because I married you. She didn't like me from the start, and you know it. She's a . . . a . . ."

"Bigot," Dad supplied.

"Yes, a bigot. And narrow-minded. But what's the use in going into that. She *is* your mother and the only living parent we've got. And even though we didn't get along at first doesn't mean I'm not concerned about her."

"I appreciate your concern. I really do," Dad said, getting up and checking his watch. "I keep in touch. What more can I do?"

Dad's keeping in touch amounted to stopping by for an hour when he was in New York for a medical convention, and phoning twice a month. I'd overheard some of those conversations. "Hi, Mom. How are you? The weather is fine. How's the weather there?" That kind of thing.

Mom opened her mouth, then closed it. She shrugged. "Do? What can you do? If you don't know, how should I?"

A lot of their discussions ended that way. Up in the air, or with one blaming the other. I ate my breakfast quickly, not wanting to be part of it. But it set me to thinking about Grandma Horowitz.

I guess she was a tiger in her day. From what I heard she hadn't wanted Dad to marry Mom. Mom wasn't good enough. Not educated enough, or clever enough. And especially, not of the same faith.

But they loved each other and married anyway. Then for years they hardly saw Grandma. Not until Eric was born, when they patched things up. Even then it wasn't often, because soon after I was born we moved to California. Now it's an occasional visit and phone calls twice a month.

Sometimes I wonder about my grandma. Dad says I'm a lot like her. Independent, with a love of music. And stubborn. At my age she'd already been working sixteen hours a day for a couple of years, in a hat factory. It's hard to imagine.

Sometimes, I think we're so rootless. One strong wind could blow the whole family down. It's as if life began with Daddy and Mom and no one came before. Whatever cousins or aunts and uncles I have live elsewhere. They're as much strangers as the people I pass in the street. I don't even know that Grandma Horowitz could add anything to our lives, but at least she'd give us a past. She'd be a root. And now especially, now that our tree seems so shaky, it would be good having more family than just Mom, Dad, Eric, and Amy.

"We're family," April said at lunch. We were all together in the Greasy Spoon, the name we give Hillcrest's cafeteria. She unloaded her tray—yogurt, a carrot salad, and a big slice of mocha-fudge cake.

"You're on a diet?" Susan asked, checking things over.

"I diet so I can eat cake." April pulled the lid off the yogurt and licked its underside, smiling without warmth. "Now, as I was saying." She turned back to me. "We are your family. You are ours. It's the nuclear family. That's how it is."

"It's easy for you to say. You have family, lots of it. Cousins, aunts, the whole bit," I said.

"Such family you don't wish on your worst enemy." April rolled her eyes heavenward and sighed.

"Why?" Being part of a big family sounded marvelous to me. Family dinners with kids to play with and talk to. People to love and hate, but because they were family, to care about no matter how angry you got. Dinners with one aunt bringing the turkey and another the pies and so on. To me it had to be better than the pleasantly dull and kind of lonely Thanksgivings at our house.

"Example," April said, forking up a big hunk of cake and dipping it into the yogurt. "Every time Aunt Rhoda visits my mother you can count on maybe ten minutes of truce before the war starts. Once she takes out her guns and begins shooting, watch out! Nobody's perfect, except Aunt Rhoda. With Mom, it's like Pavlov and the dog. Aunt Rhoda comes. Mom's mad glands salivate automatically."

I laughed and so did Michelle and Susan.

"Believe me," April said maternally, even to patting me on the arm. "You can't choose your relatives but you can choose your friends. So consider us family and friends. We're all lucky."

I took a bite of apple to hide what I really thought. In Mammoth I'd come to the same conclusion, that the only people who understood me a little were these friends. They weren't enough. As friends, we never dug deeper than the first layer. We clung to each other because we were so much alike. Brittle, cynical, and jaded. If we didn't change soon, I figured we'd petrify like that by the time we hit twenty.

"So tell me, Aunt April," Michelle said. "How does a normal teenager like me, albeit a giraffe of sorts, manage to get into such a screwed-up family? How could I have been so lucky to pull a father who goes after twenty-year-old secretaries and a mother who dates her hairdresser, and a sister who cops out by joining a commune?"

"Those are the breaks," April said in her usual smart-ass fashion. "What's the next question?"

"Aw, come on, April," Michelle begged. "That's no answer. What do I do? How am I supposed to be?"

Michelle may have exaggerated her bummed-up family, but not by much. Generally, if any of us got close to our real feelings we made jokes of it. But Michelle wasn't joking this time. She wanted answers. The answers we usually gave each other tended to be cute or useless. Maybe we avoided getting close because it might expose our own hurts too much. Or maybe we just didn't have answers for each other or ourselves.

"How do you get attention?" Michelle asked. April almost preened. She kind of shimmied up in her seat, flipped the ruffle of her 1920s blouse, and smiled. I got a sick feeling in my stomach because I figured she was going to give us one of her clever answers. Even knowing that's not what Michelle wanted, I made no effort to stop her.

"Getting attention," April said, "is something I know lots about." She leaned forward. "What you do is this: Be outrageous. Dress like a freak. Get yourself a lover. Move in with a rock musician. Flunk all your courses. Or . . ." She sat back, eyes measuring Michelle. "Or, you say f— them and pretend you're an orphan and go it alone."

Michelle let out her breath, but still seemed

troubled. I thought, Hooray, April. For once you laid it on the line. But then I realized, so? What else is new. Michelle's tried the outrageous bit. She charges clothes all over town, buys things she doesn't even need, and even gives them away. Her mother doesn't care. Her dad just groans and pays. I guess it's easier to pay her bills than pay her attention. As for going it alone, Michelle's been doing that since junior high when her dad left to marry his secretary. Maybe there just weren't answers for problems like that.

"Well!" Michelle clapped her hands together, closed up again. "So much for group therapy. Thank you, Aunt April. Now, who's got a date for the prom?"

Michelle always knew how to take the heat off herself. Because immediately, the conversation shifted. The prom was safe territory. It led to talk of who might ask whom and where to buy the best evening dress, and the like. April smirked when I said Brian had already asked me, and Susan crowed enviously. When the bell rang I realized Michelle hadn't offered a word. All during the talk about a subject she had started, she sat head bent, pulling at her cuticles. I lingered behind and fell in step beside her as we went to our next class.

"My dad's new wife is going to have a baby," she said. "Isn't that great?"

"That's wonderful," I said. Then I added, "It won't matter. He'll still love you."

"Oh, Jenny!" Michelle covered her face and started to cry.

"It's okay, Michelle. It'll be okay, really." I patted her arm and didn't know what else to say.

Driving home I went by way of Arden Road. That's where Cindy lives. Maybe I'd see her outside playing with a brother or sister, looking normal. Then I wouldn't have to phone.

Arden Road was in lower Hillcrest, the less expensive side of town. Nice, but without the half-acre lots and white two-story colonials like those on our block. The homes were closer together, the grounds not as well kept as those in upper Hillcrest. Still, it was a nice street with old trees, a sidewalk on which kids were skateboarding and dogs running free, barking.

I slowed as I neared 1294. Her home was a stucco-and-brick building with a covered entry, not very different from the house we used to live in down the block. A big oak tree shaded the ivy in front of the garage and dropped leaves on the driveway. If Cindy was home, could she be looking out the front window, I wondered, or lying down in her room, thinking?

Driving by I thought of the phone call I'd promised to make, then did something totally unplanned. I pulled to the curb, cut the ignition, and looked back, heart thumping. Why phone when here I was practically at her front door?

I got out of the car and in a moment found myself at the entry. As I rang the bell my hands began to sweat and my mind scanned a hundred thoughts. It seemed suddenly ridiculous that I should be here at all. I didn't owe Cindy a thing. She might resent my coming, even think I was snooping.

Yet, something held me there even after the third ring brought no sound of movement from inside the house. Presently I sensed a shadow behind the amber-colored glass panel next to the door. I rang again. There was a pause, then a tentative voice asked who was there.

"Jenny Hartley," I called, almost trembling.

"Jenny?"

"Yes, Cindy. It's me." In the instant's hesitation I knew she considered not opening, but at last the door moved. And there stood Cindy.

Her face was almost as white as her robe. Against that pallor her dark brown eyes, flecked with gold, seemed especially large and haunted. Perhaps she had been sleeping, because her hair curled around neck and face in disarray. All in all she seemed so vulnerable and innocent in big blue fluffy slippers and with the little embroidered alpine flowers down the front of her robe. I felt like putting my arms around her. Instead I smiled tentatively and asked if I might come in.

Without answering she opened the door wider and led the way over a small tiled entry to the living room, which looked just as I remembered, except shabbier. She motioned for me to sit on the couch, then took a chair opposite me, perching stiffly on the edge of the seat as though she might take off in an instant.

Now that I was facing Cindy, all the questions I wanted to ask seemed bold and prying. For an embarrassingly long moment we sat facing each other without saying a word. Then I asked, "Did your mother say I called? I just wanted to know if you're okay now, if you're 'well' again."

A funny little smile crossed her lips and she said, "I'm fine." Though she looked generally in my direction, it wasn't quite at me.

"Kids are asking about you, wondering when you'll be back."

A big gray-and-white cat loped across the carpeting and jumped into Cindy's lap. For a moment she just sat there, stroking the cat's back. Then she looked up and this time really met my eyes. "Do they know?"

I didn't understand her question at first because I'd been certain she must realize everyone knew. "Know what?" I asked cautiously.

"That I—you know—almost OD'd." She cleared her throat a couple of times and her mouth quivered.

"Yes, they know."

"I thought so. My mother says they don't. But that's impossible. It must have been a circus here that night, what with the paramedics and police and all that." Her voice died away and she went back to stroking the cat.

"They talked about it at first. The first day, but not much since. You know how it is. As cold as yesterday's news, that sort of thing." I tried to make light of it but Cindy didn't smile.

"I'll never go back."

"Oh?"

"I couldn't look anyone in the face again."

"It'll be uncomfortable the first day or two. Then, everyone will forget. They already have. The big news today was the prom."

Cindy pushed a strand of hair from her eyes and that funny self-conscious grin crossed her face again. I tried to figure out what it meant. It made me really uncomfortable, like she wasn't being completely honest. "We're having Chuck Seager's band for the prom, with that new singer. Billy what's-his-name? It's gonna be at the country club and later we're gonna have . . ." I stopped. Even with her head bowed that smile played at her lips. "Cindy?"

"I won't be going to the prom. You will. I'm sure. With Brian, right?"

I shook my head. "I don't know. Brian and I aren't . . . Why won't you be going to the prom?"

"Because no one will ask me."

"Of course you'll get asked."

The smile vanished. "Why don't people say what they really think? I won't get asked. You know I won't, so why make me hope by lying to me?" She gazed at me until I turned my face away. Then she asked, "Why did you come?"

"Why did I come?"

"You heard me. Why should you care? We're not friends anymore."

My face grew hot and I looked down at my hands. "It's not what you think. It's not curiosity. It's because I'm sorry. That time in the rest room when we talked . . ."

"You *knew* how much I wanted to go to lunch with you."

I winced. "Yes."

Cindy stroked the cat and watched me.

"Why did you do it? Why did you try to kill yourself, Cindy? Were things that bad?"

The smile came to her lips again and it crossed my mind that she didn't trust me. "That's ridiculous. It was an accident."

"Accident?"

"Right." Her answer sounded rehearsed. "I had too much to drink at Jan's party and felt awful, so I just went home. I couldn't sleep so I took some sleeping pills." She cleared her throat. "I guess, what with the drinking, I didn't count very well. And that's all."

I swallowed. "I guess you wouldn't understand, then, what I almost did."

She stroked the cat and shrugged. The phone rang and we both looked toward the sound. Cindy got up after the fourth ring and went to answer it. I could hear what she said. Very calmly. "Yes. I'm okay. I'm fine. Stop calling every half hour. I'm not going to burn down the house." Then she hung up. When she came back to her seat she dropped the cat on the floor. "What wouldn't I understand that you almost did?"

Asked like that I hardly wanted to tell, but some instinct made me think that it was the only way to regain her trust. And so for the next ten minutes I told her all about it. Head bent and arms hugging my stomach, I told all about how sick and lonely and disappointed in myself I'd felt these last weeks. How shallow and artificial life around me seemed. How I'd felt that last day, standing at the edge.

When I was through I felt tears on my cheeks, yet it was good, getting it all out. Through my tears I looked anxiously at Cindy. She dug into her bathrobe pocket for a wad of tissues to blow her nose. Then she jumped up and came to sit beside me, putting an arm around my shoulder. Suddenly, we were hugging each other just as we had the day I'd told her we were moving. Hugging each other and crying. Friends again.

"I feel so tired all the time," she admitted over hot chocolate later. "I've been to the doctor, but he says it's just growing pains." She stirred the liquid in her mug. "It's not that, though. It's worse. Half the time I don't even want to get out of bed in the morning."

I nodded, knowing just what she meant.

"At school, it's like I'm invisible. People look right through me. I know lots of kids, but they're not friends. Not like *we* used to be." She sipped her chocolate and looked beyond me. "That night at the party. I walked around all evening trying to—I don't know—be noticed. Connect? I stopped by one group of kids and the conversation just quit. Stopped dead, and pretty soon they all wandered off. I tried to talk to a boy in my English class and he looked so bored that I just stopped talking. Maybe I needed to loosen up, I figured, so I went to get a drink. The more I drank, the less it hurt and the more everything seemed unreal. And then suddenly I came to upstairs in a bedroom with a boy I hardly knew and I nearly threw up. That's when I went home."

She stopped and pulled her robe closer, shuddering. "I just wanted to go to sleep. To close my eyes and stop hurting. To go to sleep and never wake up."

I put my hand on hers. "Maybe it won't be so lonely anymore."

"Maybe," Cindy said, but she didn't sound convinced.

When it was time to leave, Cindy walked me to the door. She was cuddling the cat again. It occurred to me that the self-conscious smile hadn't crossed her face once since I'd told her about Mammoth. We hugged again, quickly and a little awkwardly. "I'll call you," I said. "And come back to school soon."

She didn't answer. When I reached the street and turned to wave, Cindy was still standing at the door, cat in her arms, solemnly watching.

6

The senior center was on a street near the beach, an old green stucco building with peeling paint and a new handprinted sign over the door. A wall of posters and announcements flanked the entry door telling of free concerts and lectures, of rooms for rent, used TVs for sale, bus schedules, or companion care wanted. Beyond, behind a low counter, a cheerful-looking plump woman in her sixties was typing.

"Excuse me," I said, "where do the Sunshine Seniors meet?"

"Down the hall to your left," she said, picking up a ringing phone and waving at two old women just coming through the door.

I wandered slowly down the hall, feeling very out of place. It was fifteen minutes before three, the time Solomon Katz had asked me to come. Through an open door I glimpsed about a dozen old ladies and one man exercising to a Tchaikovsky recording, eyes locked on the trim young teacher. "You are trees, tall and strong, tall and strong," she intoned, stretching upward. "A storm comes. The leaves tremble." She rippled her fingers. "Now the branches wave and sway, wave and sway."

I stopped to watch, hoping they wouldn't see me. One short, heavy woman stood legs apart like a tree planted on the floor. Her eyeglasses were fogged and her pink polyester pants strained against the bulges. She could hardly raise her arms, much less hold them straight up, and when she bent to the side, it was no more than a few inches. Most of the old people looked pretty much like that, stiff and ungraceful.

I thought of an aerobic dance class I took last year. We all wore leotards and probably no one wore bigger than a size twelve. We stretched and bounced like rubber-band balls and pretended to be members of a Broadway chorus. It was fun; hard work, but fun. The people exercising here looked hot, tired, and determined. Not one seemed to be having fun.

"Jenny! It must be Jenny!" someone behind me cried, putting a hand on my arm. "Look, Rose. Didn't I tell you?"

"So? Who else could it be? There are so many young people at the center?"

The two women I'd seen come into the center hooked arms through mine like parents of a bride. Babbling excitedly as if I were some special prize, they hauled me off to the practice room down the hall. There, Becky and Rose—because that's who they said they were—stood proudly at the door and announced, "Look, everybody! Look who we got here! This is our new accompanist, Jenny!"

I felt like running away, but instantly the half dozen or so people in the room gathered around.

"So, Jenny darling. You want I should get you some coffee?"

"No, thanks. Is Solomon Katz around?"

"You come far?"

"You remember me? You talked with me last night. Rachel Singer? You remember?"

"You're Jewish?"

I couldn't answer the questions fast enough. For this one I hesitated. What did it matter? "Well, yes —and no," I said.

"Yes and no?" They looked at each other in surprise. "A Jew is a Jew. It's not yes. It's not no."

"Leave her alone, Sara. Don't be so nosy all the time."

Why was it so important to them that I be a Jew, like them? "My father changed his name from Horowitz to Hartley a long time ago," I said.

"Why? Didn't he like who he was?"

I felt trapped. How could I answer a question like that! Yet their curiosity wasn't mean, so it was hard to take offense. They seemed to need these facts so they could decide if I belonged. So I told them about how hard it had been for Jews to get into medical schools a long time ago, which was why my dad had changed his name. Yes, they knew about that and understood. "So Daddy joined the Unitarian church."

"I would say to your father that even if he converted, he's still a Jew."

"What is this going on here, the Inquisition? Leave this poor girl alone with all your questions. You want she should never come again?"

The man who took my arm and led me away was short and sturdy with thick gray hair and dark intelligent eyes in a face so unlined, it seemed impossible he could be eighty-six. He wore dark blue un-pressed trousers and an old, rather soiled gray sweater over a shirt.

"Mr. Katz?"

"So, who else? You think Sammy Davis, Jr., maybe?"

I giggled. Solomon Katz smiled warmly. "So, Jenny, come. You've met everybody, now come meet the piano."

He led me to an old, bruised upright whose wood was polished to a wrinkled sheen and picked out the music we would use. "The piano, it's almost as old as I am, but it still plays. Sit, darling. Play for me something." He pulled out the piano bench and lifted the keyboard cover.

I played a few chords, conscious everyone was listening and watching and pretending not to. The piano was in tune, though the tone was tinny.

"It's okay, yes?"

"It's fine, Mr. Katz. Just fine."

"You should know, Jenny, some of our mu-sicians were once fine performers. Hannah, now. She played violin like an angel for the Boston Symphony."

"Really?"

"Yes, darling, really. So now we begin." Mr. Katz stepped up to a music stand in front of the room and tapped a baton on its edge. "Come, my friends," he called above the hubbub. "Sit down, sit down. Already it's after three. Soon it gets dark and we want to finish before, to get home."

One by one the Sunshine Seniors, all eleven I'd

phoned, took seats. Some needed canes, one used a walker, and everyone must have been at least seventy. Maybe men die earlier than women, because women outnumbered them nine to two.

Solomon started by making announcements. Everyone should remember to visit Sadie at the nursing home, he said. Becky would pass around a get-well card for everyone to sign. Two new classes were starting at the center, and there would be a potluck lunch to benefit Israel. Women broke in with comments on what food they'd bring and questions were asked about everything.

The first thing they did was sing. Lots of songs. All about love. I played "Somewhere My Love," "Love Makes the World Go Round," "I Love You Truly," and at least a half dozen more telling of June nights and finding old loves again. Mr. Katz cupped one hand to his ear whenever I played too softly, so pretty soon I was thumping the keys with as much zest as the Hillcrest High football team.

At last one of the men pulled out a box and began handing out the weirdest assortment of toys I'd ever seen. Penny whistles with vegetable scrub brushes stuck in the ends. A drum made of a bucket with a square of vinyl pulled tightly over the top. A bedpan strung with strings. A flower-decorated washboard played with a thimble. Even a toilet seat and cover made up to be a banjo, and a harp made from an overturned washtub!

Some of them may have been musicians at one time, but now? I wasn't sure. The piano and kazoos gave melody at least, and the rest of the toys, or whatever you'd call them, kind of clumped along for rhythm. I had to concentrate every second because the music was new to me. But now and then I'd look up to find someone grinning at me and then I'd make a mistake.

How did the real musicians stand it? We made a sorry mess of noise most of the time yet no one seemed to care. They all seemed so intent and serious about what they were doing you'd think they were playing for the New York Philharmonic. And Mr. Katz waved his baton about like Zubin Mehta.

Time went surprisingly fast. By the end of two hours we sounded much better, more like a unit, and I didn't have to play quite so loud. At last Mr. Katz put down his baton and smiled proudly. "For the first time after so long, it's not too bad, no? Not too good, but not too bad."

"Now we got Jenny to play for us, maybe we get better," a woman said.

They laughed and smiled at me, making me blush. I began putting the music away and people started to return their instruments. Two hours a week like this might not be too bad, I thought. Then Mr. Katz rapped the baton for quiet. "Please, ladies and gentlemen, one more minute, please. Rose has made the schedule. Rose darling, you will be kind enough to pass it out?"

A birdlike woman in a bright-colored dress almost danced up to the stand to take some sheets from Mr. Katz. I remembered her voice on the phone last night. Bright and youthful, full of en-

thusiasm. But what about this schedule? We prac-
ticed once a week on Thursdays and that was it, I
thought.

Rose gave me the first sheet. It read:

SUNSHINE SENIORS SCHEDULE
January–March

We meet at the center one hour before. Prompt.
You need rides or got questions, ask Solomon.

January 14 — Shalom Convalescent Hospital. 3 P.M.

January 23 — Children's Hospital. 2 P.M.

February 3 — Hillcrest Home for the Elderly. 2 P.M.

February 10 — Presbyterian Home for the Elderly.
3 P.M.

The schedule went on through March with
events set at least once every two weeks. Something
Mr. Katz had forgotten to tell me. The kitchen
band didn't play just for fun. They played to perform. It was no longer two hours of volunteer work
a week, but lots more.

I closed the piano and went right up to Mr. Katz.
He nodded and went on talking to an old lady
with a cane. "Of course, Hannah dear. I'll ask."
Hannah smiled warmly at me, then stepped aside.

"Yes, darling," Mr. Katz said. "You have a question?"

"Does this mean you'll need me on these dates,
too?" I waved the paper at him.

"Certainly, darling. We could play without our Paderewski? You know how we would sound?"

"But, Mr. Katz!"

"I understand, Jenny. You have a busy schedule. It's hard, with school and boyfriends and everything. But, darling. Think what joy we give the little ones. The sick children in the beds with leukemia and who knows what else. And the poor old people in the homes. Did you ever visit? Terrible! They sit in their wheelchairs with nothing to do. And their children never come. So what's to hurt a little music? Takes their minds from off their troubles, yes?"

"But, Mr. Katz!" In my head I was adding up the extra time. With travel and performing, it was no longer just ten hours a month, but twenty.

"Of course, Jenny dear. You can't do it? I understand. It shouldn't bother you."

I felt like a selfish child. I felt trapped and guilty. "No, it's okay. I'll manage." Without the piano the band would be chaos.

"Wonderful, darling. I knew you would. Now, could you do for me just one small little favor?"

"What?" I asked warily.

"Hannah lives by you a few miles away, maybe. The bus doesn't come so often, and the step is high for old people like us. You could take her home, darling, if it's not too far from your way?"

Hannah, standing close enough to hear, watched me anxiously. How could I say no?

It crossed my mind as I opened the car door and waited patiently for Hannah to arrange herself in

the low seat that Solomon Katz had probably promised she could ride with me even before he asked.
I'd have to watch that man.

"You got no top on this car?" Hannah asked first
thing, looking up. "You should have an accident,
it's not dangerous?"

"I drive carefully," I said, starting the engine.
She should be grateful for the ride; instead she was
campaigning already for putting the top up. Well,
it's my car, I thought. I drive it the way I like it.

"You're not cold?" she persisted, pulling her
heavy coat closer over the sweater and hunching
down in the seat. She wore a scarf over her head
under a hat, and felt cold. Unbelievable.

"No, I'm not cold, Mrs. Friedman. Do you want
me to put up the top?"

"Yes, darling, please. So we get home in one
piece."

What difference could it make at your age, I
thought, glancing over at the old lady as the top
came up. Clumsy fingers worked slowly to button
the coat. She saw my look.

"Sometimes the arthritis isn't so good and the
fingers swell so they don't even fit in the holes of the
phone dial." She shrugged. "Once, I played the
violin and the fingers, they flew." She nodded as if
it didn't really matter. "But I manage. I have my
music. I have friends. Always there are people to
talk to. I have fresh air. And I have my pigeons."

"Pigeons?" I pulled into traffic on Main Street
and moved north.

"Certainly. Every day, rain or shine, I feed them.

They expect me. I get from the store the day-old bread and they wait. As soon as I come outside, you should see!" Hannah glowed. "But enough from an old lady like me. What about you, Jenny? You got brothers, sisters?"

"An older brother and a younger sister. Do you have children?"

"Wonderful children. A son who is a doctor. A doctor, mind you! A daughter a lawyer, a son who teaches university. And six wonderful grandchildren. Everyone should be so lucky."

"Do you see much of them?"

She nodded left and then right. "You know how it is with children. They have their own lives. The doctor is so busy, even on the weekends he goes to the hospital. And the professor; he lives in Arizona. But my daughter, the lawyer, she calls me all the time. She says, 'Mameleh. Why don't you come live with us?'"

"Why don't you?"

"What would I do with myself in her big house, alone all day. No place to walk. No one to talk to. The children at school." She pulled her coat closer. "They don't keep the house warm like I like it. At night when I go to the bathroom, I'm afraid to flush, I shouldn't wake anyone. And my daughter's husband doesn't like my cooking, so I can't even help with the meals. So who needs an old lady around, somebody else for my daughter to worry about? No. It's better to have my own place, even if it is just one room."

I thought of Grandma Horowitz living in a

walkup apartment in New York, three locks on the door. Did she feed pigeons to keep busy, to feel wanted? Did she spend her time playing washboards or kazoos, praising her children and grandchildren, who hardly ever thought about her, to strangers? Here was Hannah Friedman, seventy-six, with bifocals so thick she was probably legally blind, needing a cane, fingers all arthritic, and who knew what else wrong. Living in one room all alone. *And happy!* Looking forward to getting home to feed her pigeons. *Happy!* For heaven's sake, *why?*

The "on the way" Solomon had mentioned turned out to be not so "on the way." Hannah lived a good ten minutes off my route. As if that weren't bad enough, a mile from her apartment she asked if I'd mind stopping so she could pick up some pills. The drugstore was "right on the way," so it would only take a minute. I stopped, all right, but vowed silently that would be the last time I'd take any Sunshine Seniors home again.

"I know you're in a hurry," she said, buttering me up. "So, maybe you'd go inside. With my arthritis I move so slow."

Five minutes later I walked out of the drugstore with a bag containing pills for diabetes, pills for high blood pressure, and a thousand vitamin pills. A *thousand!* Did she expect to live forever?

When I finally dropped her at her door, a two-story building much like others in the block, she invited me inside. "I'll make some tea. We'll eat some mandel bread, and we'll talk. Yes?"

No! "Thanks, Mrs. Friedman, but I really have to get home. Another time," I said.

"Another time? Then maybe next time, when you come to play, you'll pick me up first? Would it be too much trouble?"

I couldn't believe it. Brazen. No pride. I could hardly keep the irritation from my voice. "I come straight from school. I don't think I can make it."

"Well, that's okay. I don't like to make extra trouble. It's all right I take the bus. It's only one transfer." She opened the car door, put her cane outside, grabbed hold of the door with her left hand, and hoisted herself out of the seat. Standing on the street, she seemed to gather strength in her legs before she dared move. Then she put a hand on the window for support and smiled in at me. "Thank you, darling. You play good. Someday you play a concert for us, yes?"

I nodded impatiently. "Maybe. Well, gotta go. See you next week." I wished she'd take her hand off the car door and move safely out of the way already.

When she finally did, I made a quick U-turn and escaped down the street. Ridiculous! I'd volunteered to be an accompanist, not a message phoner, or a chauffeur, or a grandmother's aide. If I didn't watch it they'd have me volunteering full time in one way or another. There was a limit!

Then the picture of Hannah Friedman leaning on her cane on a rainy day, feeding the pigeons, came to me. That sickly independent, manipula-

tive, proud old lady bought day-old bread to feed
the pigeons. Because they needed her.

My God. How dare I complain!

I stopped the car and backed up. Mrs. Friedman
was only halfway to her front door, tottering slowly
up the path. She was clutching the bag of drugs
tightly under her left arm and with each step her
purse banged against the cane in her right hand.

"Mrs. Friedman!" I called through the car window. "Mrs. Friedman! Hannah!"

It took her a while to turn around and when she
did she beamed with pleasure.

"Listen!" I called. "If you still want, I'll pick you
up next week, about two forty. Okay?"

"You sure? It's not too much trouble?"

I'd have to get Schwartz to write me an excuse to
leave sixth period early. I'd have to skip going
home first for a cold drink and hope the traffic
wouldn't be too bad. "No, Mrs. Friedman, it'll be
fine. No trouble at all."

7

Every Chanukah, which usually comes a week or two weeks before Christmas, Grandma Horowitz sends each of the grandchildren the same present, money. It's always in a special envelope with a pocket, and always the same amount, ten dollars, a crisp new bill which she must get specially from the bank.

"What's ten bucks these days?" Eric said when he opened his this year. "Christ! The same amount since I was five. Hasn't she heard of inflation?"

"Never mind. Ten dollars is ten dollars. That's a hundred sticks of bubble gum and four Judy Blume books." Amy's money was gone by the next day.

Even I complained. "She could be more original. I mean—send a book, or a scarf, something personal."

"You ungrateful kids," Mom said when she heard us. "You don't deserve anything! Have you thought how difficult it is for her to send that much money from the little she has? Has one of you ever sent *her* anything?"

I usually put the money right into my wallet where it joins a lot more than that and gets spent without any trouble. Sometime in late January I get around to writing a note after Mom has nagged me long enough. I doubt Eric writes at all. And as for Amy, her note is the same each year: "Thanks for

the Chanukah gelt. We had a nice Christmas. I
hope you did, too. Love."

I once asked Amy how she thought Grandma
felt about her mention of Christmas, considering
the gift was for the Jewish holiday. Amy, always
logical, said, "I can't help it if we celebrate Christmas instead."

For some reason, when I got back from the
afternoon with the Sunshine Seniors I wanted to
write Grandma. I hunted through the mess of
papers in my desk for the envelope she'd sent. My
name and address were written in a spidery scrawl
and I wondered if Grandma had arthritis, like Hannah. And then I took out a sheet of paper, sat for a
while thinking, and finally wrote:

> Surprise! This is more than the yearly thank-
> you note. It's a hello letter. A long time ago you
> asked me to write and I promised. So here I am,
> a little late, but better late than never. So, where
> do I begin?
> First, I'll tell you a little about me. I'm even
> taller now than when you saw me last. Five seven.
> Mom says I look like Dad. Fair, with his ten-
> dency to freckle and his thick, red-brown hair that
> gets curly when it's damp out.
> Let's see—Interests. Well, I like to read. Re-
> cently I finished *The Wall* by John Hersey. Have
> you read it? Fascinating! All the time I was read-
> ing it and crying I thought—What if I'd been
> born in Poland at that time? How could I have
> escaped? The Germans wouldn't have cared a
> lick that Daddy calls himself a Unitarian; they'd
> have taken us just like the rest of the Jews.
> Which makes me wonder—what does it mean,
> being Jewish? Is it something born into you, or

is it what you come to believe because you're taught to? And what am I? Unitarian or Jewish or nothing? And is it important to know?

I didn't mean to get so philosophical. Where was I? Oh, yes. Interests. Well, besides reading I like music, playing piano and flute, and listening to records. Dad says I inherited my musical interests from you, that you used to have a fine voice. Do you play any instruments?

Friends. Ah, there's a good subject. I have a lot of friends, yet not really one good one. I don't know why that is and it's very depressing. You need someone to tell your true feelings to who will listen and not make fun or tell you it's stupid. Know what I mean?

I have a boyfriend, Brian. He's good looking and popular. We hardly ever go anywhere that someone doesn't know him. Brian's really sharp, a go-getter, as Mom would say. He'll probably be a millionaire by the time he's twenty-one because everything he gets into turns to money. I'm not criticizing him, mind you. Money's fine. Except sometimes it seems like that's all he cares about.

School. Kind of boring, but okay. Wish I knew what I wanted to do with my life. Probably go to college; everyone does here, whether they want to or not.

It's too bad we live so far apart. It would be nice to be a whole family. Have you ever thought of moving out here? Tell me about your life, Grandma. Before and now.

Thanks, by the way, for the money. This year I'm putting it aside to buy something special. I don't know what yet, but when I do I'll write. Meanwhile, I'll sign off. Please answer soon.

> Love from your grandchild,
> Jennifer.

For a long while I sat there staring at the letter, thinking. It would seem strange to Grandma, hearing from me like this. Would she be pleased? I wondered what she'd say about Cindy, if I could ever bring myself to write about that.

After addressing the envelope, I went to my purse to take out Grandma's gift, the new ten-dollar bill. Until I wrote the letter it hadn't occurred to me to do anything special with the money. Now I knew I'd like to save that bill for something I'd remember as being possible because of Grandma. Ten dollars didn't buy much, as Eric said, and maybe it seemed a bit silly, even sentimental. But that's what I wanted to do. I folded the bill twice, then slid it into a secret compartment in my wallet, smiling to myself and feeling oddly pleased.

"Tell me about Grandma," I said to Dad after dinner, going to sit on the arm of the wing chair where he was reading.

He looked up from the medical journal in his lap, his mind a million miles away. "Hmm?"

"Tell me about Grandma. Were you close when you were growing up? Where did she come from? How did she meet Grandpa? Things like that."

Dad put the journal aside and looked at me in surprise. "Do you really want to know?"

"Yes, really."

"Then bring me that brown leather photo album from the study, the one on the third shelf, to the right."

I jumped up and went into the study. Mom used to be conscientious about pasting up photos of our growing years and family vacations. She stacked the albums side by side on a high shelf so we couldn't pull them down and crayon them, as Amy did one year. It had been a long time since she'd added albums.

I carried the book to the game table, blowing the dust off the top while Dad pulled out two chairs on rollers. "It's been so long since I've looked at these," he said, running a hand slowly, lovingly, over the embossed leather cover. There was a shyness, an almost reverent attitude toward what he held.

"What are you doing?" Amy called, coming into the room.

"We're going to look at photos, princess," Dad said.

"Mom!" Amy shouted. "Mom, come see. Daddy's showing old pictures."

Soon we were gathered around the album. Years ago our family used to do things like that. Look at slides together on winter evenings, and play Monopoly or Probe together. When we played Monopoly, Daddy used to steal from the bank and look wide eyed and guiltless when we accused him. Then, if we all ganged up on him, he'd say, "As father of the house I have my rights." Eric was best at Probe because he'd come up with words I'd never heard of like "arcane" or "seminal." I'm still not sure what they mean.

"Now, this," Dad said, peering closely at a black-and-white dog-eared photo, "was Grandma as a girl." He passed the album to me. Amy and Mom crowded close to look over my shoulder. The photo showed a slender, solemn-eyed child in an ugly tank-type bathing suit that went to her knees. Two laughing boys stood on either side of her. "Mother used to say her brothers had just flattened a sand castle she'd spent two hours building; that's why she looks so glum."

Grandma's engagement picture especially interested me. According to the date below, it had been taken when she was eighteen. Grandpa Horowitz stood stiffly to the side and slightly behind Grandma, who was seated. I wondered what he'd said just before the photographer snapped the picture because Grandma looked as though she could barely control a giggle.

"Oooh, what a funny dress," Amy exclaimed. "So fussy, so many bows."

"Wasn't she pretty," Mom remarked wistfully. "And isn't it terrible what time does to us."

"You asked how they met, Jenny," Dad said. "It was quite romantic. Mom's father owned a resort hotel in the Catskills. That's outside of New York City. Mother was expected to help out around the place as well as to entertain the guests in the evening; she had a lovely voice."

"Yes, she did," Mom echoed.

"Dad came up one summer for a week's vacation. He worked in New York for a brokerage house. Fresh from Sheffield, England, and as proper and straitlaced as a stick. Right off he fell for Mother. She liked him, too, but she didn't give him the time of day. She'd been warned to stay away from the eligible bachelors. The women guests had first dibs."

"What's dibs, Daddy?" Amy asked.

"Rights, honey," Mom answered.

"Then how *did* they get together?" I asked.

"One thing about your grandfather," Mother said. "He never gave up on what he wanted." She put her hand on Dad's shoulder.

I made a mental note to ask Grandma in future letters more about that.

For the next hour we pored over the pictures, including one of Grandma holding Daddy when he was only a few months old. Most of the later photos were of Dad's brothers and sisters growing up. But here and there you'd see Grandma and Grandpa, five years older, or ten. She'd been taller than most women of her generation but with the years seemed to shrink. And the head of heavy, dark hair which had been tied in a fashionable bun in her engagement picture became a short bob and later a halo of soft, wavy silver around the head of a little, fragile old lady.

"It's such a sense of—*going on*," I said, searching for the right words to say what I felt. The photos had touched me in a strange way. They showed Grandma growing up, falling in love, marrying, having children, and growing old. And it showed her children beginning that same cycle.

"Continuance, going on," Mom said thoughtfully. "Yes, that's what it is, and it wasn't easy." Daddy had told how poor they'd been during the

Depression, of Grandma's illness, of Dad's oldest brother dying in the war, of Grandpa's business failing, of his long illness and death.

"What made it worthwhile was their love." Mom looked directly at Dad. "They had a glow about them I'll always remember."

Dad closed the album and gave it back to me to put away. Amy went off to her room. As I left with the album I glanced back. Mom and Dad still sat at the table leaning toward each other, talking quietly.

Saturday night Brian picked me up to go to a party at April's house. She called it New Year's II "for all those unfortunates who celebrated the New Year away from Hillcrest."

"Dress up and be prepared to toot in the year with a vengeance" were her instructions.

Parties used to be such fun, so exciting. I'd nearly fall apart just waiting for the day. From the minute the invitation came I'd start planning what to wear, wonder who else might be there, plot how to get someone I liked to notice me.

But there'd been *so many* parties! Lately they all seemed so alike. Same kids, same things to eat and do. Same dumb jokes and nothing conversations. Just the thought of going to one more made me feel irritable and trapped.

Then why go? There were a dozen excuses I could invent, even if it was April's party. Because, I realized with a sinking heart, I don't know how to say no, which is another problem with me. I need to be loved so much I always do what other people

want, and say what others want to hear. Example: I
don't really want to go to a fancy private college.
The state university would be just fine. But Dad
wants me to go. Mom wants me to go. That's why
I've kept up the grades. That's why Schwartz got
me into the Sunshine Seniors thing. Because I'm a
good girl who hasn't the guts or imagination to do
her own thing.

Look at my relationship with Brian, I thought.
Except for this week when I balked over the car
race I've never seriously disagreed with him. He'd
be annoyed. I'd feel rejected.

What would happen, I wondered, if for once I
did what I really felt like doing? Said what I really
thought? I'd probably lose all my friends, or they'd
say I was stoned. Well, be different for a change, I
told myself. Try it. You can't hate yourself any
more than you already do. And April's party is the
perfect place, and time, considering the New Year,
resolutions, and all that.

April lives in an ocher-colored, tile-roofed villa,
behind iron fences and an electronically controlled
gate. The house is so big that a party held at one
end wouldn't be heard by people living in the other.
Not that April's parents would likely be at home;
her Dad's an international banker and is more
likely to be in Zurich or London than Hillcrest.

"Dahlings," April greeted, a cigarette in a long
holder between her fingers. "So glad you could
come."

Brian squeezed my hand and laughed. "Who are
you today, April? The Duchess of Windsor?" April

wore a short 1920s flapper dress and black patent-
leather shoes with bows. Her wiry red hair, usually
in need of trimming, was held in place by a satin
band. Around her neck she'd draped a long, feathery
boa.

"My dear, if you have to ask . . ." April raised
one eyebrow at Brian and sneaked a glance at me
to see if I found her funny, too. April no longer
shocked me; she was always trying on new per-
sonalities. Maybe she didn't like hers any more
than I liked mine.

"Happy New Year, dahling," I said, going along
with the act and giving April a quick hug.

Brian's interest had already shifted to who was
there and what was going on. He loved parties and
could hardly wait to get involved.

"Well, isn't this *great!*" He gestured at the bal-
loons and crêpe paper, at the kids dancing or hanging around the bar, at the band in the corner.
"You'd never know it wasn't New Year's!" He hurried me over to a marble table where most of the
kids had left their wraps. I dropped mine on the
pile. "April took my advice about the music, I see.
Great!"

The band he was referring to didn't sound great
to me. In fact, it was awful. The drummer wore a
sleeveless undershirt and his arms were full of
tattoos. One guitarist had shaved his hair like a Hare
Krishna and the other's hair was purple. I like rock
and country music, even good jazz, but what we
heard was noise.

"They're gr-*eat!*" Brian repeated, leading me to the bar and smiling proudly. "It's the Dark Side. I signed them to do three gigs!"

"They're terrible, Brian," I said quietly, uneasily. "Just listen."

"Terrible? You're crazy! They're the most popular group in Hillcrest, Jenny. Where ya been?"

"Right here in Hillcrest. Same as you." I gave him back the same unfriendly look he gave me. "And just because they're popular doesn't mean they're gr-*eat!*"

Brian dropped my hand. He looked at me as if I were some unpleasant shade of green. "I think you're spending too much time with the old folks, kid. Either that or you don't know the first thing about music."

"It's not music, Brian. Honestly. All they're doing is cashing in on their weird look. That's what they're selling, not music." I couldn't stand his stern, superior air. "And don't call me *kid.*"

By this time we'd reached the bar. Brian put on his hearty "friends of everybody" smile and made some cracks to a couple of our friends, but he was mad. He ordered drinks from the bartender, handed me mine, then turned away as if we were strangers. He'd done that to me once before when I'd hurt his masculine ego. Tonight he'd probably act as if he hardly knew me, play up to other girls, then come back to me at the end of the evening as if nothing had happened. Well, he could play that game all night for all I cared. I wouldn't let it bother me. I joined some of the kids nearby and put on my "having a great time" look. It wasn't easy. I felt cold and sick inside, and wished I could go home.

"If you could be anybody beside yourself, who would it be? Quick! Answer the first thing that comes into your head!"

"Brooke Shields."

"La di da!"

"A Ram quarterback."

"Godfather III."

"Dracula! Aaargh!"

About eight kids, including Susan and Michelle, sat on the rattan couches and chairs or stood around having fun with the question.

Susan caught my eye, looked past me for Brian, I suppose, then asked, "How about you, Jen?"

Actually, I didn't know. Anybody, except myself, I supposed, so I threw out the first names that entered my head. "Eleanor Roosevelt. Gloria Steinem. Sylvia Plath."

"Eleanor Roosevelt, jeez! Ever see pictures of her?"

"Sylvia Plath? Who's she?"

"Oh, she's that poet. Didn't she commit suicide?"

My face grew hot and everyone looked at me so I changed the subject. "How about you, Michelle? Who would you be?"

Michelle rose to her full height and tilted her head at a haughty angle. In a deep, dramatic voice she said, "An actress or a model." Amazingly graceful, she pirouetted and walked as she imagined a model would.

"Not bad, not bad! I'll buy that one!" someone said and everyone started laughing.

It began getting dumb so I drifted away. Maybe I'd just get my coat and go home. But I couldn't. Brian was driving. I'd have to wait until he was ready and he looked as though he wouldn't be until everyone left. Across the room I saw him leaning over Lila Brown and she seemed just as hungry for him. Good for them. In fact, GR-EAT! The noise was beginning to give me a headache.

I was heading for the door to the terrace, not even stopping for my coat, when someone behind me said, "He's not very smart, you know."

"What?" I turned, startled, to face a tall, thin boy with thick reddish hair, intelligent eyes, and a generous mouth. He was holding a plate heaped with cocktail tidbits and smiling. "Have one. They're really good. I recommend the quiche. And these little things wrapped in bacon. And this and this." He laughed. "I guess I recommend them all."

"Who's not very smart?" I asked, ignoring the food.

"Brian. You're his girl, aren't you? If you were my date, I wouldn't leave you alone for a minute. So, I guess he's not very smart."

"That's a good line." I turned back to the door.

"Wait, please." His voice changed, became serious and less self-assured. "I'm not much good at this sort of thing. It was a line. I was working on it for the last ten minutes hoping to get the chance to use it. I figured that's what someone like Brian might say."

"Are you for real?" I closed the door and looked back at him.

"The truth is, I'm not very comfortable at parties like this. Don't even know how come April asked me. She's in my history class and out of the blue she comes up to me and says, 'Paul Bernstein'—that's my name, by the way—'how would you like to come to my New Year's party?' And I say, 'New Year's was last week, so are you talking about next year?' And she says, 'That's what I like about you. You can read.' And I say, 'Why me?' and she says, 'Why not you?' And I don't know what all this talk shows except that when I'm ill at ease I run off at the mouth."

He smiled and popped another hors d'oeuvre into his mouth. "Have one before they're all gone. Come on." He held the plate out again.

I took the rumaki, the bacon-wrapped thing he loved best. "Don't you know anyone here?" I asked. Over his shoulder I glimpsed Brian maneuvering Lila into a dark corner. I moved slightly so Paul blocked the view.

"Not a soul, except by sight. You're Jenny. I know that because I asked. I know something else about you because I eavesdropped."

"Oh? And what do you know?" I smiled. Paul's shy grin made me feel warm and happy.

"You don't like the band."

"Oh, boy! Are you ever right! Do you?"

He laughed. "It's awful. In fact, it's awesomely awful." He gazed around the room. "But I'm terribly impressed. This kind of party astounds me."

"Why?" Among the boys I knew, not one would admit something so naive. I suppressed a smile.

He leaned forward and dropped his voice. "I'm kind of used to a simpler life. Parties with chips and colas and the Stones on a tape deck. But this! Phew!" He gestured with one hand. "Do you know there's a room back there with a hot tub and a dozen guys in it, in the buff?"

I knew. That was supposed to be one of the advantages of parties at April's house. Brian and I had gone in it a few times, but always with bathing suits. Not all my friends were so modest. "No kidding!" I said.

"Bartender, caterers, waitresses, a band! Can you imagine what that costs? And most astounding is that with all that, nobody seems to be having much fun. I mean, look around. Half the guys are drunk already and the other half are working at it."

He was so on the mark that I became defensive.

"Very perceptive. I bet you have a part-time job after school, get straight A's, and run track."

Paul got very red in the face. "I do have a job, but I'm into basketball, not track. Are you laughing at me?"

"Not at all. I'm just seeing the difference. You're right, of course. We are a bunch of rich, spoiled brats. We feed off our parents and all we ever think about is having a good time."

"Jenny, hey! I didn't say— I wasn't trying to— You're not like that, anyway! I heard you back there when you said you'd like to be like Eleanor Roosevelt!"

"I talk a lot. Saying isn't doing. You can always tell a person by the company she keeps."

Paul Bernstein opened his mouth, then closed it. For a moment I feared he'd reverse himself, deny everything he'd honestly perceived. I'd have hated him if he did.

I don't know what gets into me sometimes. I'll meet someone I really like or admire and suddenly turn flip like I want them to hate me. That's what I did then. For the next few minutes I babbled on about some of our crowd's crazier doings. Like the contest to see who could hold the most booze. Like the time the guys put snakes in the girls' toilets.

Watching his face I could actually see him slowly withdrawing. From that nice warm grin it changed to a puzzled frown and then went blank, like he didn't dare reveal what he thought of me.

That's when Brian showed up. Protecting his property, I figured. "Nice meeting you," I threw over my shoulder as I walked off on his arm. Paul nodded and didn't answer. I could feel him watching me all the way to the dance floor. I felt stupid and angry and ashamed.

8

All that the girls talked about Monday morning at the Greasy was April's party. Susan picked over each of the couples who came. Michelle wanted to know what anyone knew about Paul. April asked, "How come you didn't go home with Brian?"

"Because he spent most of the evening with Lila to punish me." I took a sip of apple juice and checked out the kids coming into the cafeteria. Someone had said Cindy was back.

"Punish you for what?"

"For something I said. Hey! There's Cindy!" I stood up. "I'm going to ask her over."

"Wait a minute," April said. "I don't want her here."

"Why not?" I asked, hands on the table, but watching Cindy. She was making her way between tables, holding a lunch tray.

"Because she's not one of us. Because we're talking about *my* party, and she wasn't there. Because she makes me feel uncomfortable."

Every table Cindy passed was either crowded or the kids seemed unusually absorbed in eating and talking. Cindy moved along slowly, face flushed, like she didn't really care. Then she turned and started to the empty tables on the edge of the Greasy.

"I'm going to ask her. If the rest of you feel the same as April, tell me now."

"Oh, come on, Jen. It wouldn't be the same with her here and you know it," Susan said.

Michelle squeezed ketchup onto her burger, then licked a finger. "I don't care. Do as you please."

April glared at me.

"Okay. No offense. I'll go sit with her instead." I slung my purse over my shoulder and picked up my tray. "See you guys. Tah-tah."

By the time I reached Cindy she had set her tray down at the opposite end of a table from two other kids and was setting out her foods. Each plate or container had to be placed just right, almost as if she were working an intricate puzzle.

"Hi, Cindy, mind if I join you?" Without waiting for an answer I set my tray down opposite her and slid onto the bench.

"Aren't you afraid of contagion?"

"Huh?"

With a nod of her head to the rest of the kids in the Greasy she said, "I feel like a leper. I never saw such a large-scale turning of backs. My God! You'd think I was invisible!"

"They're just embarrassed. They don't know what to say to you."

"Well, my God!" She glanced furtively at the two kids at the end of the table and lowered her voice. "I just want to be treated like a normal human being, that's all! After all, I didn't hurt anybody except myself! And it was an accident, anyway. I just took too many sleeping pills. It was an accident."

She avoided my eyes, so I picked up my ham sandwich and began eating.

"You don't believe me!"

"Oh, sure, I do. Why shouldn't I?"

She readjusted her milk carton and moved the Spanish rice plate a quarter of an inch to the right, then a half inch to the left. Her hand trembled when she raised the fork so she put it down and hid her hands under the table.

It was lucky that the loudspeaker clicked on with announcements from the office, because I didn't know what to say or do. Cindy didn't want me to see how angry and embarrassed and ashamed she seemed to be. And to tell the truth, if I'd been in her place I'd have felt the same. In fact, I'd want to transfer to another school rather than face people who didn't know how to talk to me anymore. And I could easily have been in her place.

As soon as the loudspeaker went off I tried to think what to talk about that would be neutral and safe. "Guess what I'm doing Thursday afternoons?" I asked brightly.

Cindy picked up her fork and stirred the rice about.

"I'm playing piano for a bunch of Jewish senior citizens. You should see them. They look like escapees from an old-age home. And the music they play reminds me of the band we had in kindergarten with the triangles and maracas and stuff." I paused. Cindy didn't seem to be listening. "There's a woman named Hannah I drove home last week.

Can you imagine? She rushes out to the bakery each morning to get day-old bread so she can feed the pigeons! Isn't that weird?"

What kind of beast was I, making fun of those nice old people just to get a smile out of Cindy? I began to wish I'd never left my friends, and turned to sipping my apple juice. It tasted tinny and warm, but it filled the silence until I could think of something else to say.

"Cindy?" I began again. "I've got ten dollars to spend from my grandmother. She sent it for Chanukah. You didn't know I was half-Jewish, did you? Well, *was*, till Dad converted. If you had ten dollars, what would you spend it on?"

"I have so much work to make up," Cindy said softly, not answering my question at all. "My mother will be furious if I don't get all A's."

"So what if you get a B? It's not the end of the world."

"Oh, yes, it is! I've got to get into a good college. I've got to! I can't disappoint her." Cindy was becoming agitated, fidgeting with the fork and then the knife, not seeming to know which one to pick up and use.

"Your mother will understand. After all, you've been out of school all week. It's hard."

"Finals are coming up. I have two papers to write. I'm barely keeping up in math." Cindy moved the milk carton a fraction of an inch to the right. "I don't see how I can do it!"

"Look. I'm pretty good at math. If you like, I'll come over and help. Really, you'll catch up."

She shook her head and her lips trembled.

"Why not?"

"It wouldn't work. I can't concentrate any-more." She pressed her fork down on the Spanish rice, making crisscross patterns. "Lately I can't seem to understand what I read. I sit at my desk and stare at a sentence and read it over and over again and it doesn't make any sense." Her voice dropped. "It's hopeless."

"Maybe you should tell your mother," I said, thinking how little it helped to speak with mine.

"No, it won't help. I'm too far behind. I'm never as good as she wants. I'm not smart enough, or pretty enough, or nice enough, or popular enough, or anything enough for her."

What should I say? *You're just depressed. It will pass.* But maybe it wouldn't. "Maybe you should see a doctor. A psychologist . . ."

"No. My mother would worry what the neigh-bors would think, and my father." She shook her head. "No."

"Cindy." I reached across the table for her hand. It felt cold and damp. And then the bell rang and she pulled away.

We left the Greasy together, not talking. Before going our separate ways I offered her a ride home. "I take the bus," she said, head bowed.

"Then would you like to go shopping with me tomorrow to buy something with my grandmother's gift money?"

"I don't know. Maybe." She said it as if she already knew she wouldn't but didn't want to hurt my feelings or get more questions.

Watching her walk away as though she didn't really know where she was going, my heart ached for her. Whatever hopelessness I'd felt seemed worse in Cindy. And how could I help her when I didn't even know what to do about my own self? What could I say or do? I didn't know.

As soon as I turned around to head toward government class on the second floor, there was Brian. He knew my schedule because we'd exchanged programs months ago. In the good days between us, he'd walk me to nearly each class, then hustle to get to his own room before the bell rang.

"What do you want?" I asked rudely as he fell in step beside me.

"Ah, come on, Jen. I just want to talk. Don't be like that. You're making such a big thing out of nothing."

"Brian, I'll be late for class. I don't want to talk about Saturday night."

"Listen! You spent the whole evening with that guy Paul, didn't you? So what are you mad at me for?"

I stopped in my tracks and just looked at him. Now he was trying to turn everything around, make me the bad guy when it was he who had abandoned me. "Oh, boy," I mumbled and started walking again.

He hurried after me. "Lila doesn't mean a thing to me. You know that. I just got angry because you made fun of the Dark Side. And you know what? You were right. They are bad."

"Wonderful."

"Ah, come on, Jen. Don't be that way. I'm sorry. I made a mistake, okay?"

"And what happens the next time I don't say what you want to hear?" My throat tightened but I forced myself to sound as normal as possible. Brian and I were pretty close, if you know what I mean. It's not so easy to break off something like that, especially when the other person still claims to care. But I felt all mixed up inside. If you couldn't tell your supposed closest friend what you really felt and thought, then what kind of closeness did you really have?

We were at the door to my class and the second bell had already rung. Brian held my arm. "If we disagree, we'll just work it out, okay?"

"I don't know, Brian."

"Say, I saw you at the Greasy with Cindy. She okay?"

Now, where did that come from, I wondered.

"And listen. Why don't I drive you to that senior center Thursday. Then afterward we can go out to eat together."

How nice. He was in trouble with me so now he asked about things he'd never shown interest in before. He didn't care a bit about Cindy. He could hardly wait to change the subject when I'd first told him about the senior center. I pulled my arm away. "I'm going in, Brian."

"Thursday?"

"I don't know. Maybe." Cindy's words and tone. But Brian didn't notice. The last thing I heard as I entered the room was him saying, "Gr-eat!"

As I pulled out of the parking lot after school, I slowed, trying to see if maybe Cindy was in line near one of the buses. But it's not easy to find anyone. The buses hide the kids and there's so much traffic that the best you can do is be sure you don't run somebody down. I drove off, telling myself she probably wouldn't have come with me anyway.

All the same, I felt down again. I felt really scared and worried about Cindy. And bad about Brian, because I didn't intend seeing him again and didn't know if I could really handle that. When I reached home I ran straight to my room. Threw down my books and fell on the bed. And suddenly, I was crying.

"Oh, yes, Jennifer. Do come in. Cindy's in her room. Down the hall to the left."

Mrs. Bickford greeted me a shade too eagerly, as though Cindy never had friends stop by. And with relief, as if her daughter's problems could be transferred, now that I was here. Still, she didn't seem hard or mean, like the slave driver Cindy described. But then, how can you ever tell. People often behave one way with strangers and another with their own kids. Take my own father. You'd think he was the most thoughtful, considerate man in the world if you saw how he dealt with his patients. The way he listens and watches, I bet everyone thinks Dr.

Hartley worries so much about them that he even takes the worries home.

At home, it's the opposite. Dad hardly notices what's going on. He may ask, "What's up?" but he doesn't really want to know. Then, as soon as you start talking you can see his mind closing down and drifting away elsewhere. Maybe he *is* thinking about his patients.

Cindy's room was as stark and unadorned as a cell, which was just the opposite of how I remembered it from sixth grade. Then, you could hardly see the walls for the colorful posters, and the worn carpet was always strewn with games and books. Now I had a feeling of darkness and cold. Cindy's bed still stood in the corner, but the chest of drawers and her desk were so neat you'd think no one used them. The white walls held a calendar and a wooden, evil-looking mask. A Mexican rug covered part of the floor. Its fringes lay so straight, they looked combed.

Cindy lay curled in a ball on her bed, asleep. I crossed the room wondering if I should wake her, but as soon as I reached her bed her eyes flew open, wide and scared. She sat up quickly.

"Gosh, I didn't mean to frighten you," I said softly. "But remember yesterday? I asked if you'd like to go shopping with me. Rather than phone and maybe get turned down I thought I'd just come get you."

"What? Oh, Jenny." She rubbed her eyes.

"Come on. Get a jacket. It'll be fun," I said, looking around for a closet.

She shook her head. "No, thanks. I'm awfully tired." She hugged her stomach and rocked back and forth.

"Oh, come on," I said heartily. "It'll do you good. Where's your closet? I'll get a jacket."

"*That's right, Cindy!*" I heard from the door. "This business of napping afternoons is ridiculous. There's no reason for you to be tired. The doctor checked you out and there's nothing, absolutely nothing wrong with you."

"Mom . . ."

"No, Cindy. I mean it. You ought to be making up all the work you missed instead of sleeping so much. Now, get yourself up As long as Jennifer is here, well—why don't you go off with her for an hour? The fresh air may do you good."

Cindy pushed herself up and went to her closet. I was sorry I'd come, now. Maybe she would be better off asleep. From the doorway her mother watched us both, arms crossed tightly over her bosom. I couldn't tell if she was angry or concerned, or maybe both. She followed us out of the room and waited until we climbed into the car. "Good-bye," she called. "Have fun!" I waved, but Cindy just looked straight ahead.

"Okay, now," I said after we were under way a few minutes. "As my English teacher would say, 'Let me reiterate.' My grandma, who lives in New York, sent me ten dollars for Chanukah. Each year I kind of lump it with other money and it gets spent. On gas for the car, food at the Greasy, you name it. Well, this year I want to buy something special, something to remember her by. Get it?" I glanced sideways to see if Cindy was listening. She was. The fresh air seemed to be helping because her face looked less chalky. "Okay. So, what can I buy that's 'memorable' and only costs ten dollars?"

"A Rolling Stones album."

"Yeah!"

"Two coupon books for dinner at McDonald's."

"Good, but not memorable," I shot back. "Two seats at a Charlie Chaplin flick."

"A subscription to *Playgirl* for six months."

"Hey, that's a good one! African violets. That's grandmotherly."

And so we went, trying to outdo each other. Smiling and then even laughing. Really laughing. It felt so good to find I could still do that, even though what we were saying wasn't all that funny. Cindy laughed really hard, and then suddenly she was crying. With one hand I worked my way into my purse and found a packet of tissues which I dropped on her lap.

After a time she blew her nose and wiped her eyes and snuffled a little. "Well, that felt good." She smiled through reddened eyes. "Now, where should we shop?"

"I thought Maggie's. It's expensive but maybe I can find one perfect little thing. And anyway, I'm headed that way."

"You can't buy a safety pin there for under ten dollars," Cindy said, "but what the heck. Why not."

Maggie's is Hillcrest's most elegant boutique. Everything about it spells money, from the thick carpeting to the scent of Italian leathers and French perfumes. The salespeople speak in British accents and dress as though they buy at Maggie's, too. Maybe they get discounts on discounts.

A doorman opened the car doors and an attendant drove my Porsche away. "You'll have to tip him," Cindy whispered. "Does that count as part of the ten bucks?"

"Ssh!" I nudged Cindy as we entered the store. "Everyone charges here. Money is considered dirty!"

For the next half hour we wandered and browsed, talking in looks and whispers. For twenty-five dollars and up you could buy a silk scarf so filmy and light it might float on a breeze. I fell in love with a green and off-white mohair shawl from Ireland ($175). The jewel case held tiny gold charms that would have been perfect for a bracelet but the chain on which the charms would hang cost more than Grandma had sent.

"What about that ivory heart?" Cindy asked, pointing to a small, perfect heart on a black velvet background in the display case.

"Yes, that would be perfect. Miss? May I see that, please?" It was so small I figured it couldn't cost much.

The saleslady unlocked the case and lifted the tiny heart out, laying it on a square of wine velvet. "Ivory is very rare now, you know. That is an old piece."

I glanced at the tag and showed it to Cindy. She let out her breath. "On the other hand," she said after a moment, "you really had something a bit more expensive in mind."

We left quickly after that, going out the back door to the parking lot as if we'd just stolen something. "Maybe we should try Ohrbach's basement," I said. "My brother was right. You just can't buy anything for ten dollars, anything special that is. Maybe I should just get some stationery."

"No, wait. There's a store on Third near Fair Rose. It's almost a junk shop, but it has all sorts of fascinating things. I was there last year; let's look. You never know."

Third near Fair Rose wasn't a part of Hillcrest I knew well. When you drove through you'd see men in black suits and round, flat hats, and curls hanging down in front of their ears. Food markets opened to the street and chickens hung from hooks in the meat markets. People carried food in string bags and talked together in little groups in Yiddish or poor English, and strange music blared out of the record shops. I'd read about *shtetls*, little Jewish villages in Eastern Europe a century ago, and that's what it seemed like to me.

"If your grandma's Jewish, you must be at least part, so maybe you'll find it interesting from an ethnic point of view." Cindy eyed me anxiously, then looked away.

I don't know about this Jewish thing, or about being any religion for that matter. In my own thinking, it doesn't matter what you are, how you worship, or who. All that counts is being a good person and not hurting anybody. And yourself included. While I didn't always obey that rule, it pretty much summarized the extent of my religious feeling. More not to offend Cindy than out of any real interest, I drove to Third and Fair Rose.

The shop Cindy led me to was indeed different and strange. You'd hardly notice it in passing because the windows weren't very clean and the store itself was so narrow and dark. Inside, display cases lined the walls and the place smelled musty and oddly spicy. Mr. Cohen, the owner, sat in the back on a stool, bent over a book. He didn't even look up when the little bell over the door announced us.

"We'll just look," Cindy said, sensing my reluctance. "Just five minutes and then we'll go." She drew me farther into the store.

The cases held boxes and trays full of old things, things you wouldn't find in department stores or places like Maggie's. Rings and necklaces, bracelets and belts, like pieces you might see in museums. In minutes I became so fascinated that we stayed not five minutes, but an hour.

Mr. Cohen pushed down the embroidered yarmulke he wore on the back of his thin white hair. Tall and stooped, he came to us, book still in hand and smiling.

"They're beautiful," I said softly. "Where are they from?"

He held up a lacy silver necklace with tiny colored dangling beads. "Now this one I got just last week. It comes from Bukhara. Do you know where that is? It's in Russia, near Afghanistan. The family who sold it to me emigrated just last year. It had been in their family for a hundred years."

The silver looked like the patterns of frost on a window in winter and I touched the delicate pieces carefully.

"And these are Yemenite."

I tried on rings shaped like coiled snakes and a necklace Cleopatra might have worn. There were earrings and pins from Eastern Europe, the last cherished jewelry from families who had escaped Hitler, sold when the parents or grandparents passed away because "It is the new and shiny the young want today," Mr. Cohen said.

I felt awed, touching and trying on the valuables of Jewish people who had lived a long time ago in faraway countries. I tried to imagine who had first worn each piece. A dull, gold pin with rubylike glass especially pleased me. It came from Poland, where my great-grandpa was born. Mr. Cohen could not recall how it had come to him. And I wondered how its first owner had felt on seeing it for the first time. Had her husband given it to her on their wedding day? Did she wear it pinned to a high-necked blouse and pass it down to her daughter? Was it ever used to bribe some border guards so the children of that daughter might escape to America?

"I like this a lot. How much is it?" I asked, holding the pin out. Mr. Cohen brought the faded price tag close to his thick glasses and told me.

"Oh." I looked at Cindy, disappointed. It was more than I would spend.

"It has to be ten dollars, no more," Cindy explained. "She's buying it with money from her grandmother."

"So maybe you find something else you like."

"No. I don't know why, but this is what I love," I said.

"So, in that case, we make an exception. It's not so important I make a profit. How often do I meet two such beautiful ladies who make me wish I could be young again." Mr. Cohen began packing it, placing it on a sheet of tissue paper, folding the paper and taping it closed. No fancy box. No pretty ribbons. An awkward bundle.

"So, enjoy." Mr. Cohen handed me my grandmother's gift. "And come back again. You don't have to buy." Before we were even out of the door his head bent over the book again.

Cindy and I left the old shop smiling. It had been an odd and satisfying afternoon. Driving home I felt a special bond between us. And again I thought how odd that I had come to help Cindy and instead had received from her more than I had given. "I could come over tonight and help with your math," I offered when we reached her home.

"Thanks, Jenny; that would be nice." She smiled, a really warm and happy smile which made her look especially pretty. "I'm glad you made me go."

"Great," I said. "In fact, gr-eat!"

She didn't understand why I laughed, but it didn't matter. She laughed along with me.

9

Before getting out of bed each morning since Mammoth I'd lie still awhile listening to myself, sort of taking my emotional temperature. Would I be able to get through the day without wanting to go off someplace and cry, and without feeling as if the whole world lived on the other side of a thick, impenetrable glass?

The morning after I saw Cindy I woke feeling anxious and scared. Not for myself this time, but for her. Though she had left me yesterday smiling, the work together that evening had not gone at all well. I'd explain a math problem that was really easy and she'd nod and pretend to listen but you could tell by her eyes that nothing was sinking in. In the few hours since I'd dropped her off she'd withdrawn again and there was nothing I could say or do to help.

Didn't her parents see what was happening? Why didn't they get help for her? Could they really believe that story about taking too many sleeping pills accidentally?

At breakfast Mom said that Brian had called and would phone again. I wondered what he could want now and made a face.

"Where were you, anyway, last night? With Brian?" she asked.

"No." I poured juice into a glass and brought it to the table. "I'm not seeing him anymore. And I was at a friend's house, helping with math."

"What happened between you two?" Mom asked.

"I just don't like him much anymore. Maybe I never did. Dad?"

"Mmmm." Dad didn't look up from the newspaper.

"What would you do if you thought a friend of yours might try to kill herself. Or *himself*," I added to throw Mom off the trail.

"Hmmm?" Dad said, then I guess it sank in because he looked up and added, "Why do you ask? Do you know someone like that?"

"Maybe."

"Jenny, I told you," Mom began, but I ignored her.

"Dad, what would you do?"

He put the newspaper aside. "Why do you think that? Has she spoken about killing herself? Does she drop suggestions that she'd be better off dead? Has she talked about giving away any of her things?"

"Well no. At least not to me."

Mom, Dad, and Amy were all watching me, waiting for an explanation. "She OD'd on sleeping pills and said it was an accident, at first, and I don't think it was because later she said when she took the pills she never wanted to wake up. And she's really depressed. Sleeps a lot. Can't concentrate. Lost weight. I don't know. She just doesn't seem right."

"I told Jenny she should stay away from her," Mom said to Dad.

"Anyone who tries suicide needs help," Dad said. "Have you talked to her about it?"

"A little. She said her mother always makes her feel like she's never smart enough or pretty enough or anything enough. She thinks no matter what she'll never be able to measure up."

"Now, that's silly," Mom said. "Did you tell her that?"

"It's not silly to her." Dad didn't take his eyes off me. "What did you say?"

"I really don't remember. Not much, I think. What should I have said?"

"I'm a cardiologist, not a psychiatrist, but you don't say 'It's all in your imagination.' That much I know. The best thing to do is listen well and show understanding."

"How?"

"Well, you might say, 'I know you think your mother doesn't love you and it must be hard to love yourself when you feel like that.' Or maybe, 'I understand how boxed in you must feel.' Something like that."

"Could I be wrong? Could it have been accidental?"

"Do you think so?"

I hesitated. "No."

"Then trust your intuition. And ask her."

"Ask her?" Mom said, outraged. "Why, that's ridiculous. If she didn't have the idea before, you'd just be putting it into her head!"

What Mom said made sense. How could I actually come right out and ask Cindy such a question? I looked to Dad for confirmation.

He glanced at his watch, sipped a last mouthful of coffee, and got up. "There's nothing at all wrong in coming straight out with the question. Something like 'How long have you been thinking about killing yourself?' She'd be glad to have the chance to tell someone. Just sharing those thoughts helps defuse the pain." Dad gave Mom a quick pat on the shoulder, told her he'd not be home for dinner, and said, "Gotta go."

I jumped up and followed him. "Dad, wait! What if she does admit she's planning—" I left the sentence unfinished. "And swears me to secrecy, what then?"

"Then, Jenny dear," Dad said, putting on his overcoat, "you say, 'Okay, I promise not to tell.' " He paused and gave me a penetrating look. "And the second you get the chance you run like hell and tell her parents what she's up to."

Daddy opened the door, looked back, and winked. I watched the door close, stood there thinking over what he had said, and finally went back to the breakfast room.

Came lunchtime I settled at my old table in the Greasy determined to include Cindy in the group this time, April willing or not. But so far she hadn't shown.

Trying to talk above the usual lunchtime hubbub wasn't easy, especially when Mr. Hart got going with his captive-audience announcements. "Try-outs for *The Music Man* at three thirty today! Come on, everyone; let's see some school spirit and turn out. Hillcrest *Log* staff will meet at the journalism room immediately after sixth period. . . . Cross-country meet Friday at Oak Grove Park. Come on, everyone; show your support and turn out." And so on.

Michelle fingered my new pin. "Interesting, very interesting. Where's it from?"

Interesting was Michelle's diplomatic word for what she didn't like or hadn't quite made up her mind about. "Got it from a secondhand shop yesterday when I went shopping with Cindy."

"Looks old and valuable," Susan said admiringly.

April gave it a cursory glance. "Looks old and junky. Bet you didn't pay more than ten bucks for it."

"Thanks a lot!" I shot back. "You should know, if anyone should!"

"That's right. Just call me Queen of the Secondhand Shops." April smiled and looked around the cafeteria. "Where's your little friend, anyway? Stringing up a noose in her garage?"

Susan tittered uneasily and watched us both. Michelle dug into her lunch pretending not to have heard.

"That's not funny April," I said. "Cindy told me it was an accident."

April snorted knowingly, then cocked her head toward the loudspeaker over which Mr. Hart was repeating his announcements. It provided a fortunate lull in what might have turned into a nasty argument. It hadn't occurred to me until then that April's cynicism was the glue which held us all together. She made us feel superior by cutting down everyone else. Why I'd bent to her leadership so readily I don't know, but I vowed to myself I wouldn't anymore.

"You know," Michelle said, breaking the uncomfortable silence, "it might be fun to try out for *The Music Man,* don't you think?" She glanced at April for approval.

"You worry me, Michelle, you really do. You've got this image of yourself as a kind of Sarah Bernhardt and you're not, you know."

Michelle stared mutely at April, twisting a paper napkin into cones.

"What part did you think you'd try for?" Susan asked. "The schoolteacher? You'd be too tall, you know. They could never find a male lead tall enough."

Pow, right in the gut, I thought. "Rubbish! Try out if you want to, Michelle. What can you lose? Who knows, you might even snag the lead!"

"Michelle get the lead?" April snorted again and shook her head. "That'll be the day."

"Sure! Why not?" I was just about to add, Boy, you're sure bitchy today, when Michelle interrupted with "You're probably right that I'm too tall, and it doesn't really matter. Probably wouldn't be much fun anyway."

If Cindy had come into the room at that moment I'd have kept her away from the table for sure. To bring her there would be like leading a lamb to the slaughter. When you've already climbed into a coffin, you don't need "friends" to come along and hammer the lid closed.

"Hi, Mrs. Friedman," I said when I picked up Hannah Thursday after school to drive to practice. "How are you?"

"How am I?" Hannah carefully lowered herself onto the bucket seat, suppressing a flicker of pain. Porsches, I thought, were not for the elderly. "I'm fine. When you don't break a leg, you could call yourself fine. So? And you?"

"To tell the truth, not so good," I admitted, pulling away from the curb. "I broke up with my boyfriend. I'm having second thoughts about my friends. And I'm worried about a girl I know who may be suicidal."

"About the boyfriend and friends, it's not so terrible. You can always find others. But about the suicidal. Oy vey! Such a thing to even think about! A young person, yet."

"What do you mean, a young person yet? Don't you think we get depressed?" I kept my eyes on the road, not wanting her to see how important her answer was to me.

"Depressed, certainly. Everyone gets depressed. You think I don't cry when my body is falling apart right before my eyes, worse each day? You think, when my daughter doesn't call for two weeks I don't feel depressed? But to kill yourself, no. Even in the concentration camps when the people were skin and bones, they hung on. And you know why?" Before I could answer she said, "I'll tell you. Because they had a goal." She nodded vigorously to emphasize the point. "No matter how sick and starved and miserable they were, they made themselves get through one more day, and one more. You know why? For the goal!"

"What goal?"

"To live. In spite of the Germans. To spite the Germans. To sleep in a bed with clean sheets again. To hold in their arms their wives and children once more. To see that their torturers were punished."

I didn't say anything for a while, thinking about the movies I'd seen of concentration camps. It had always seemed too horrible to be true. Starved men with shaved heads in striped pajamas peering through barbed wire fences. Children with huge, swollen bellies lying in big pits with hundreds of dead, naked bodies around them. Smoke coming out of crematoriums. "I never knew anyone who was in a concentration camp," I said, sounding doubtful.

"No?" Hannah peered at me closely. "You don't know Solomon Katz?"

"Sure, I know Solomon Katz."

"Then you know someone."

"What?"

"You didn't see the numbers burned on his arm?"

"Mr. Katz?"

"Yes, Mr. Katz. But he was one of the lucky ones. He came out alive. The rest, his wife and children, his mother and father and all his sisters and brothers, they weren't so lucky. So, now you know."

I almost went through a red light, and jammed my foot on the brake. Hannah braced herself on the dashboard and chided me for driving too fast. How could it be, I thought. Mr. Katz seemed so normal, so happy.

"You want he should cry forever?" Hannah replied when I asked. "That kind of sorrow, Jenny dear, you don't wear on your sleeve. You keep it buried deep inside, in your heart. Life goes on. And you keep on guard that it won't happen again."

I opened my mouth, then closed it again and for the next minutes became absorbed in making my way through the traffic. Such a strange conversation to have with a near stranger. In all my years I'd never discussed anything like this with my family or any of my friends.

We were almost to the center and I found myself wishing there were miles more to drive, because once we arrived the subject would be dropped. So I said, "Mrs. Friedman?"

"It's Hannah, darling."

"Hannah? What do I tell my friend? She has lots of goals. But they're not her own. Or maybe they don't seem very important to her."

"So Jenny, what you really ask is this, yes? What's the meaning of life."

"I guess."

"And the answer is, you shouldn't ask."

I must have looked disappointed because she said, "You're not satisfied? That's not good enough, my answer?"

"Well . . ."

"So, all right. You live because God put you here. And it's up to you to make something good. You go to school and learn everything you can, and you get a job and do the best you can, and you marry and bring up children and teach them to be responsible. And you help people not so well off as you and if people they take advantage of others, you don't turn your head away." She smiled a little. "And maybe even, you feed the pigeons. In other words, darling, you don't question. *You just live.*

"I could say, it's a sin to kill yourself. Do you believe in God?"

"I don't know."

"In the Jewish religion, there's a saying: When you kill someone you kill not only that person but his children and his children's children. Maybe, too, an Einstein?"

I nodded. It was something to think about.

"You want I should tell you a story?"

"Sure."

"So, here goes. When Methuselah he reached the age of nine hundred years, his son begins to worry when would he be ready to die. So he goes to his father one day and says, 'Pa? Today it's your birthday. You're nine hundred! So? Nu? What about it?' And Methuselah, you know what he says? He says, 'Oy, my son. Don't rush me. I'm still a young man yet.' "

I laughed and Hannah laughed as we pulled into the parking lot at the center. I helped Hannah from the car, waiting until she straightened herself and felt ready to walk on, then said, "Thanks, Hannah. Really, thanks."

"Thanks? For what?" She seemed pleased but embarrassed, and shook off my helping hand. "So anyway, you're welcome."

Together, with painful slowness, we made our way into the center.

10

Thursday after practice I came home all keyed up. We'd had a lot of fun, really. Everyone tried extra hard because our first performance was set for Tuesday at a convalescent hospital. One of the women, Faegl, I think, played a "corsetina," which was nothing more than a corset strung with rubber bands. Solomon and Becky sang a duet together, "I Love You Truly." It brought tears to my eyes to see the sweetness between those two, little Solomon and big Becky.

"Dinner's ready," Mom called up.

"Down in a minute," I answered. Then I picked up the phone and dialed Cindy. My afternoon was just the thing to tell her about to cheer her up. And especially, I wanted to hear what she thought about Hannah's philosophy. But as soon as I pushed the buttons, the same funny uneasiness crept through me as it had the first time I'd phoned. How would she react? Would she be hard to connect with? Would she be up or down or what?

"Oh, Jenny!" her mother greeted. "How nice! Cindy's in her room, working like a beaver. I'll get her." In a lower voice she said, "You just don't know how much you've helped her. I'm so grateful!"

Wasn't there a *Mr.* Bickford? Wouldn't he be grateful, too? While I wondered about Cindy's father, she came on the line. I kept my tone light but all my antennae were up. "Didn't see you at school today. Playing hooky?"

"I was there. You just didn't see me," she said. "Spent lunch hour at the library trying to make up what I missed."

"You did?" My sweaty, cramped grip on the receiver eased. "Well, swell. How's it going?" She sounded perfectly normal, even happy.

"It's going fine, Jenny; much better, in fact. If I keep at it through the weekend I should be pretty well caught up."

Nothing at all about trouble concentrating. No quaver or suppressed tears. It made me wonder if maybe I'd made a big thing out of nothing. Maybe Mom was right about hormones, after all. I let out my breath in a relieved sigh. "Want me to come over tonight to help with the math? I've lots to tell you about the senior group. And I had this remarkable talk about life with this old woman."

"Oh, Jenny, thanks, but not tonight. It's going well and I don't want to do a thing until I'm caught up. I've kind of set myself a deadline, too."

"Oh." I felt both relieved and disappointed.

"Say, Jen, you know that ivory heart you saw at Maggie's that you liked so much? Well, I've got one almost like it and I want you to have it."

"Oh, no, Cindy, I couldn't. That cost forty dollars!"

"It's only money, and I hardly ever wear it. Please? Say yes."

"No, really." It would make me feel uncomfortable accepting such an expensive gift.

"You liked it, didn't you?"

"Yes, sure."

"There! You said it. I'll drop it by this weekend."

She seemed so pleased I couldn't say no, so I thanked her and swore I'd love it, then offered to stop by if she was so busy studying.

"No, don't. I'm really snowed. I'll be over Monday."

"Okay, then. See you Monday."

"Sure."

"Have fun, then."

"Studying?"

I laughed. "I'm glad, Cindy, that everything's okay again. See you at school. Bye."

"Bye, Jen," Cindy said. "Be happy."

I hung up and let out a deep breath. Cindy would be all right. She'd catch up on her work, then we could do things together, share how we felt, be real friends. Maybe she'd even like to volunteer at the senior center so we could drive there together.

Friday night after dinner I sat at the piano playing music I hadn't tackled in a year. Liszt's "Hungarian Rhapsody," for example. Now, there's a piece that's really beautiful. Full of spirit and unexpected playfulness, but very hard. Four sharps and whole lines where you play bass clef with both hands. Still, my fingers seemed to remember where to go after a while and I just sat there playing.

I'd have to play it for Cindy. When we were friends before I moved I'd been taking lessons only two years and most of the music I played was at the level of Dick and Jane.

My mind was so far away that I hardly heard Amy. She tapped me on the shoulder, then tugged at my arm.

"Jen? Are you deaf? I'm bored. Let's go to the mall."

"Go away. I'm busy," I muttered. "Read a book."

"I don't want to read! I got my allowance and I want to go to the mall to play Pac-Man."

I ignored her but made one mistake after another. Amy tugged at me again. "I'm hungry. I want a pizza. Let's *go!*"

I stopped playing and glared at her. "You just ate. Now, don't be such a brat. Go a-way!"

Amy backed off a foot. Tears brimmed in her dark eyes and her tone lost its whine. "Jen," she pleaded. "It's lonesome with no one to talk to. It's scary in this big house. I hate Friday nights."

"What's scary? I'm here. The doors are locked."

She looked down at her feet, not answering. Suddenly I realized that Amy spent most Friday nights alone. Mom and Dad always went out to dinner and then to play bridge with friends and I was usually out, too, with Brian or the girls. It hadn't occurred to me before that Amy minded being alone. Poor kid. She had her problems, too. I closed the piano lid and got up. "Okay, sweets. Sure. Go get your jacket," I said. "And let's go."

* * *

Hillcrest's shopping mall was even lonelier than home. With the holiday sales over and the spring things not put out yet, the mall felt like a place in Future World. Our footsteps echoed on the marble floors as we walked the two blocks to the game arcade. Salespeople stood at the open fronts of their shops watching us silently, but they seemed unreal, almost like the manikins in windows. Even the music sounded too loud, and though the climate is controlled, I felt cold.

With only two others in the dark arcade it felt evil with its blipping, clinking electronic voices and blinking consoles. Amy didn't mind, though, and very quickly forgot all about me. When I left, she was leaning into a dark machine, tongue out, eyes glued to the lighted screen and hands busily twisting knobs as tiny spaceships raced across the panel.

For a while I wandered aimlessly in and out of shops, just looking. It's something I've done hundreds of times, yet that night it felt wrong. I browsed through the paperbacks at Waldenbooks and followed the scent of cookies baking to the Chipyard. Then, tired, I sat in one of the social pits on a wooden bench facing a shoe store.

Nibbling a cookie I didn't even want, I looked around and thought, What are we doing here? Why aren't we home in a warm, friendly house with our parents around? Then I thought about Hannah and a story she'd told me of her childhood Friday nights.

"The house was warm and clean and smelled of all the wonderful foods my mother had cooked that day and that we would eat together as a family later," she had said. "I'd stand beside my mother, dressed in my best clothes, my hair freshly washed and braided. And she would light the Sabbath candles. Three times she would circle the bright lights with her hands as she said the prayer. Then, she would turn to me and take my face in her hands. 'Good Shabbos, darling,' she said. 'Good Shabbos.' Every Friday night. I would feel the warmest, happiest joy in my heart like I never felt any other time. Even to this day."

That was Hannah's childhood Friday nights. This was mine, sitting in a near-empty shopping mall waiting for time to pass. It made me feel so alone, so hungry for home and family and closeness that I nearly cried. I left the cookies in the bag on the seat and nearly ran back to the arcade.

"Amy, come on," I said, taking her firmly by the arm. "We're going home."

She seemed so mesmerized by the game she didn't even hear me until I said it again.

"Home, no! One more game!"

"No more. Come on, let's go. I've got a surprise for you."

"Surprise? What?"

I took her by the arm. "It wouldn't be a surprise if I told. But it's something very special I learned about from that old lady I met, Hannah."

That, Amy couldn't resist. After only one trial whimper she followed along beside me on the way home. I went straight to the kitchen pantry and knelt down to search behind the six-packs of diet drinks for what I vaguely remembered having seen years ago. Brass candlesticks given Mom by Grandma Horowitz when she married Dad.

"Are you getting *Cokes*?" Amy whined. "You tricked me. I could have bought drinks at the mall."

"Not Cokes, Amy." I found what I wanted and stood up to show them to her. "Candlesticks."

"What fun are those?" She backed away from the tarnished, dusty sticks. "They're yucky!"

"Not after we clean them up. And wait till you see what we do with them."

I rummaged among our cleaning supplies and brought out rags and brass polish, then Amy and I went to work. We rinsed off the years of dust and grime and then applied coat after coat of polish. Little by little the warm, burnished color of the brass showed through.

"These candlesticks," I told Amy as we worked, "came from Grandma Horowitz. She hoped Mom would light them every Friday night like *she* used to do when Daddy was growing up."

"Why?"

"Because it was a tradition. The whole family would gather for dinner together no matter what, on that one day of the week, and lighting the candles started the celebration of the Sabbath. And you know what? Grandma's mother lit candles in these holders when Grandma was growing up—in a little town in Poland. And her mother before that."

"How come Mommy doesn't?"

"I guess she doesn't believe in it. She says half

the troubles in the world started because people fought about religion."

"Then why are we doing it?"

"Because it feels good to be part of the past this way. Now, go find the matches, while I get candles."

I found the special candles. Not the fancy, spiral ones Mom used so often, but short, simple white ones that must have been in their box behind the Cokes as long as the candlesticks.

"Okay, Amy," I said. "You can have the honor. Tear out a match, close the book, and strike it here."

In a moment the candles were lit. Set on the white cloth of the dining room table, the candles in their holders appeared stately and beautiful. In the flickering light the brass gave off a warm glow.

"Now what?" Amy asked, looking at me. "What did Grandma do next?"

"I'm not really sure. I think Hannah said something about putting a cloth on her head and saying a prayer. But I don't know the prayer."

"Make something up. Let's pretend it's olden times and we have a big family, and we're all going to have dinner together after."

I smiled. "Okay." I bent my head and thought for a moment. Then I said, "Dear God. These candlesticks haven't been used in a long time and no blessing has been said in this house before. But tonight, by lighting these candles, my sister and I want to connect with all the family that came before us." I paused, wondering what else to say.

"Thank you, God, for good health. And for giving us each other. Amen."

"Amen," Amy echoed. Her eyes sparkled. "Now what?"

"Since we already had dinner, we'll have tea!"

We had our tea and cookies and afterward played Scrabble. Instead of turning on TV I read to Amy from *The Wind in the Willows*, a book I'd loved at her age.

"You know, Jenny," Amy said before going off to bed. "This was a really special night. Much nicer than being at the arcade."

"You don't say?" I said, giving her a playful punch.

"Yes, I do say."

"Well, that's good. I'm glad!"

Later, as I prepared for bed, I thought of Amy's words and of the closeness lighting the candles had brought us. Maybe next Friday I'd try to prepare a Sabbath dinner. Hannah would know what to make. I'd ask her, too, what the proper prayer was. Or, maybe I'd call Grandma and ask.

"What are Grandma Horowitz's candlesticks doing on the buffet?" Mom asked the next morning. She was on her way out to the country club with Dad, for tennis.

"I thought they were yours now."

"Don't be smart. You know what I mean. What are they doing out?"

"Hannah Friedman, the old lady in the senior

band, told me she lights candles every Friday night, so I thought I'd try it. Why? Is there a reason I shouldn't?"

Mom gave me an odd look, then looked to Dad for support. "Lighting candles on Friday night is a lot of religious mumbo jumbo. Anyway, what's all this sudden interest in religion and that sort of thing?"

"Cool it, Liz," Dad said softly. "You know how kids are at this age. Don't make a big thing of it."

"If you don't want them on the buffet, I'll put them in my room," I said.

"No, you won't. It's not like trying on my shoes when you were five years old. These are heirlooms, not toys."

I felt like saying, Heirlooms shouldn't be kept at the bottom of a kitchen cabinet, but there was no use arguing. If Mom didn't want the candlesticks out, I'd put them away. That didn't mean I wouldn't take them out again next Friday night. Maybe every Friday night.

Mother watched me for one more moment, then threw her tennis sweater around her shoulders and turned away. "I don't know, Phil. All this interest in old people; it's becoming an obsession."

"Today old people, tomorrow something else," Dad said as they left the room. Then I heard him humming the tune from *Fiddler on the Roof*, the one with the chorus, "Tradition, tradition!" And Mom laughed.

Just before they left I heard the mail drop

through the front door slot and then silence as Mom or Dad picked it up. Then Mom called, "Jenny? A letter for you. From Grandma Horowitz." You could tell by her tone she wasn't exactly pleased. "I'll leave it on the hall table." And then the door closed.

11

"Jenny dear," Grandma wrote, "your letter gave me such joy. Like sunshine. Of course I will write, as often as possible."

She wanted to know what I studied at school and all about our family. In answer to my questions she said she loved opera, especially Verdi's music. "So much heart he had, so beautiful." She spent her days reading, mostly novels of old Russia, although her vision was becoming poor. "I hope you won't laugh at an old lady like me, but the best time of the week is when I go to the junior high and help with the children who can't read. Last week I couldn't go," she wrote, "because like a dummy I tripped and hurt my back. But don't worry. There is food in the house and by next week the back will be better for sure."

I read the letter again, then thought about it. What if Grandma's back didn't get better so fast? What if she ran out of food, or needed a doctor? Would anyone look in on her? How sad that Grandma's two children lived so far away—Aunt Joyce in South Africa and Daddy in California.

By the time Mom and Dad came back the only thing I could think was that they had to do something to help Grandma.

"Whoa! Hold it!" Dad exclaimed when I blurted

out my fears. "Take it slow. Just exactly what did she say?"

I showed them the letter. "She needs somebody, Daddy. I've seen how hard it is for Hannah to manage and they're about the same age. Daddy, please, you've got to do something."

"I'll telephone."

"Phil . . ."

"What!"

"Jenny's right. She's getting too old to be alone."

"Now, don't you get on my back. You and my mother get along like cats and dogs. What do you want me to do? Bring her here?"

"No, no, of course not! That's not what I meant at all!"

"Then what did you mean?" Dad bellowed.

"I thought, well, maybe you could fly back East . . . and look around for . . . a retirement home. You know. A nice place. Not one of those awful places like . . ." She stopped at the look on Dad's face, and they stared at each other until Mom looked away.

"You know, Phil. There comes a time when *you* have to decide what's best for her. Joyce isn't around to help and if she can't care for herself, then *you* have to make the decision."

"Hey! Wait a minute!" I cried. "You said Grandma doesn't want to go to a 'home.'" All of a sudden I was afraid of what I'd started. "Why can't she come out here?"

"No way," Mom said.

"Why not?"

"Jenny, you stay out of this. If she comes out

here, it will be me who'll be saddled with the problems, not you."

"Can't you forgive, after all these years?" Dad asked.

"Forgive, yes. Forget, no. But that's not the issue."

"Then, what is?"

"I will not have your mother living with us. I'm all thumbs around her. It just wouldn't work. Even if she didn't say a word, I'd feel she disapproved."

"But, Mom! She doesn't have to live here. I could ask Mr. Katz and Hannah Friedman. They probably know of apartments near the beach. She could live there and go to the center. She'd have a life of her own and we could still watch over her."

"It's a good suggestion, princess, but it's academic," Dad said. "You don't know your grandmother. She's a stubborn old sweetheart, set in her ways, and she doesn't like help from anyone."

"Then don't offer help. *Lie* to her. Tell her that *we* need *her*."

"The egg teaches the chicken," Dad said. "You may have something."

"We do need her. It wouldn't even be a lie." If I put into words what I felt Grandma's being here could mean to us all, even to Eric, it would sound corny. I almost held my breath as I watched Mom.

"It might work," she said doubtfully. "But not in this house."

"Daddy?"

Dad shrugged. "No harm in asking. It's not like we haven't thought about it often enough, but

maybe now's the time to push. I'll lay odds, though
—she'll refuse."

"When? When will you call?"

"Jenny, now, stop it. Honestly. You don't know
when to quit. Your father will call and talk to her
and let you know. Okay?"

"Okay." I did my best not to jump up and down
as Amy would and left the room without another
word. If Grandma did come maybe it wouldn't
change our lives that much, but it might. Already
she'd drawn Mom and Dad closer somehow, not
only through the photo album, but now, as they
planned together. It was really exhilarating, fight-
ing for what you wanted. Maybe that was the magic
formula, after all.

Ten minutes later I dialed Grandma from a pay
telephone in town. It would be five o'clock in the
afternoon in New York. Even if her back was better, she'd be home. Old people stayed home after
dark; that much I'd learned.

"Yes? Hello?" Grandma's voice sounded a bit
anxious, suspicious, as if phone calls weren't usual.

"Grandma? This is Jenny."

"Who? Jenny?" She hesitated. "Jenny, my grand-
child?"

"Yes, Grandma." I found myself smiling. She
had such a small, frail voice. "How are you?"

"My goodness, child. Where are you calling
from? Are you all right?"

"I'm in California, Grandma, and I'm fine. But
how are you? How's the back?"

"Not so good, but it'll be all right. A little Infrarub, the heating pad, and soon I'll be good as new."

"Have you seen a doctor, Grandma?"

"Doctors are for sick people. Me, I have only a little pain. Nu? Who doesn't? That way I know I'm alive."

I laughed.

"My back is not so interesting. You're calling from California, from a phone booth yet. I heard all the coins dropping. What's so important you shouldn't call from home?"

"Oh, Grandma," I exclaimed, surprised at how perceptive she was. "The truth is you're going to get a call from Mom and Dad later and they'll ask if you'll come out here to live."

"That I can't do," she answered after a moment. Stiffly, I thought. "They asked me already, years ago. I said no."

"But years ago maybe it was different. Now you need us and we need you."

"You need an old lady who can't even lift up her feet high enough she doesn't fall? Like the chicken pox you need! No, darling, I see what you're trying to do. You think because I hurt my back I can't take care of myself anymore, but you're wrong. Even with the back, down the hall I help Mr. Simon. Don't worry, I manage."

"Of course, you do, Grandma. I didn't mean it that way." She was insulted. I was surprised at the catch in my voice and angry with myself for not being more diplomatic and persuasive. "Grandma! We do need you. I do. And Amy does, too. Even Mom and Dad, though they don't know it. And Eric."

"Jenny darling. It's sweet you should say that, but how could that be true? You have out there everything, sunshine, good health, a nice home, each other. What more could you need?"

"I don't know, Grandma." My throat tightened up and tears suddenly seemed very close. I swallowed a couple of times and waited a moment, trying to think. Then I said, "We need you, Grandma. We need to be, to be—kind of glued together. And maybe you can do that." Again, I stopped and waited for the pain in my throat to ease. "We don't know who we are, Grandma. Sometimes it's like we're . . . like the shopping malls. All plastic and modern and cold. Grandma? Do you know what I mean?"

I imagined that Grandma nodded. "But how? What could I do?" she asked.

"I'm not sure, Grandma. But it seems to me you've got something we don't. You *know* things. You . . . believe in things. You . . . know who you are and what you came from. You . . . I don't know . . ." I ended lamely.

For a few moments neither one of us spoke, then I said, "They don't know I'm calling, Grandma. Will you come if they ask you?"

"I don't know, darling. I couldn't say yes and I couldn't say no."

"Even for a visit, just to try it," I pleaded.

"I'll think about it, Jenny, but I can't promise."

Monday morning before school I went outside to put a letter to Grandma in the mailbox and found a small, wrapped parcel inside addressed to me. It was from Cindy. She must have left the gift on Sunday, but why hadn't she come to the door and knocked to see if I might be home? Was she that busy catching up with her work that she couldn't spare one minute?

I unwrapped the package and found the small ivory heart she'd spoken of and a folded paper with only two words: "Be happy." In my room I found a gold chain to pull through the tiny gold loop on the heart, then fastened it around my neck over a red sweater. It looked beautiful. So pure and perfect against the cashmere. I could hardly wait to get to school to show Cindy and tell her all about Hannah and Grandma.

It was a gray, cold morning with a fine drizzle. Driving to school I thought how on other days like this it had taken enormous willpower to get out of bed and start the day. But today, despite the weather, I felt sunny and warm inside, full of good intentions and hope. It was such a nice feeling, I wanted to hold on to it.

"Guess what?" Michelle greeted when I met the girls on the school steps. "First period's canceled. We've got special assembly instead."

"Yay!" Susan cried. "I miss an algebra test."

April yawned and mumbled something about getting some sleep because special assemblies were so boring and the four of us ambled into the auditorium together to find seats.

You could tell immediately what was on because

the stage was set up with folding chairs and music stands. And then I remembered that the school orchestra would be performing at a state competition next week, so this was probably their dress rehearsal.

As the orchestra members filed out of the wings with their instruments I felt a small pang of regret. I could have been up there with them. I'd wanted to try out for orchestra way back in freshman year, maybe playing flute since they could only use one piano player. But April had said, "Who needs it? They're a bunch of nerds." And I'd caved in when Michelle reminded me there'd be practice afternoons while they were out having fun. A lot I had to show for three years of "fun."

"Hey, look who's in orchestra!" Michelle pointed out a girl we both knew carrying a violin case onstage and a boy from my French class lugging a bass fiddle. And then suddenly Susan cried, "Isn't that Paul?"

"Paul? Where?" Almost immediately I saw where she meant. He was just coming out of the wings, a tall, dark-haired girl beside him. They both carried flutes. The girl leaned toward him and said something and he smiled.

I glanced to both sides to see if the girls noticed my interest, because they could so quickly make fun of things like that. But Susan was bent over a paperback romance and April had dropped off to sleep.

What with everyone talking and visiting back and forth and the orchestra tuning up, it was really noisy. But I hardly noticed. The only people who interested me were Paul and the girl. She sat beside him, pushed her hair back, and lifted the flute to her lips. Paul moved the stand so they could share it and pressed the music sheets flat. Then he sat down and unpacked his flute. Finally Mr. Barnes came out and everyone quieted down. He bowed to the audience, then turned his back to us.

They played for a half hour, all kinds of marvelous pieces, like Beethoven's "Egmont Overture" and "Rodeo," by Aaron Copland. It was not only marvelous to hear, but a pleasure to watch. Each musician bent over his instrument almost lovingly or sat waiting, listening, while others played.

They were so good! Even April woke up and sat straight. Like a perfect rainbow of musical colors. When it was over, I let out my breath as if I'd been holding it all that time.

"Aren't you coming?" Michelle asked as the lights went on and I remained in my seat.

"No, just go on. I'll be along in a minute."

As the auditorium emptied, musicians began packing their instruments and leaving. Soon only a few boys remained, folding the chairs and stacking them along the side of the stage. One was Paul.

I wished he'd notice me. I wanted so much to tell him how good they all were, to make up somehow for the bad impression I'd left him with last time we'd met. Slowly I got up and started walking to the stage. The boys were joking back and forth, too busy with the chairs to look up. About twenty feet away I called, "Paul?"

One of the boys nudged Paul and pointed. "Who's there?" he asked, coming to the edge of the stage and peering over the footlights.

"It's me, Jenny. Jenny Hartley."

"Jenny?" He shaded his eyes. "Just a minute, I'll be right down." With that he jumped off the stage and came striding toward me.

"Hey, what are you doing here?" he asked. "Did you like it?"

"It was wonderful. Really wonderful," I said.

"Yeah. We're not half bad." He grinned happily. "We might even have a chance at first place."

"I didn't know you played flute," I said. "I do, too."

"Really?"

I nodded and laughed, gripping my books as though my life depended on it. All of a sudden I felt so awkward, like a kid talking to a boy for the first time.

"Well," Paul said. "Thanks for the kind words. I'll tell the others. Better get back to the chairs now."

"I guess I better go, too," I said, but neither one of us moved, even when the bell rang. "Maybe we can play something together sometime," I added, backing away. "Music, I mean." I blushed. "On our flutes."

"Yeah," he said, walking backward toward the stage and smiling. "Call you sometime."

I couldn't quite get Paul out of my mind all morning but didn't want to talk to the girls about him. At lunchtime I scanned the Greasy for Cindy, but she wasn't there. April was explaining, off-handedly, that her parents were away again, to Zurich this time, and wouldn't be back for six weeks. Her eyes looked especially tired, as though she weren't sleeping well again.

"Goodness, didn't they just get back from China?" Susan asked. "How long were they home this time?"

"A week."

"Must be awful, alone in that big house so much," Michelle said. "Would you like me to stay over sometime? Mom is out nearly every evening, anyway."

"I'm not alone," April said defensively. "We have plenty of help, you know, two maids and a cook and others who don't live in. But if *you* feel lonely, Michelle, you're welcome to stay with me. We have fourteen bedrooms."

Michelle glanced my way and suppressed a smile. "Thanks, April. I'd love to come. Tonight?"

"Well, sure. That would be fine." April seemed to perk up right before our eyes. "How did the play tryouts come out?" she asked Michelle, without a shade of malice in her tone.

Michelle blushed and looked away. "I got a part, not the lead, but a nice part with fifteen lines!" She could hardly keep the delight from her voice, unsure how April would respond.

"Well!" April said. "Fancy that! If you got a part, maybe I should have tried out!"

It was the closest April had ever come to an apology or compliment. The tone encouraged Michelle, who started talking about the need for help in staging. "With your experience in finding unusual period clothes," Michelle was saying when I got up to leave, "maybe you could get on the wardrobe committee."

I didn't stay to hear April's answer because with ten minutes until next period I thought I'd check out the library for Cindy. Which is exactly where she was. Sitting in a corner with her back to everyone, she was writing furiously in a looseleaf notebook.

"Cindy?" I touched her shoulder. She jumped.

I pulled out a chair and sat down. She really looked good, bright and alert and even happy. Her glance went to the ivory heart, then to me. "Looks nice on you," she said.

"I really love it. Thanks again, but why didn't you ring the bell and give it to me personally?"

"No time. I have this deadline. I told you. This is the last report to finish, then I'm caught up."

"Then let's get together and talk. I have so much to tell you. How about tonight?"

She looked evasive. "Not tonight."

"Darn! Tomorrow I have the senior citizen thing after school and I'll be busy afterward. Gosh, we're up to Wednesday already. Do we have to make appointments just to talk?"

She smiled. "It's all right. It can wait. I know you've been worried, but you don't have to be anymore."

The bell rang. I glanced up, annoyed, and got up. "Aren't you coming?"

"Just have to finish this. Another minute." Her head bent over the page again.

"Wednesday then?"

"Ummm," Cindy said.

I touched her shoulder.

She gave me an abstracted nod and mumbled, "Sure."

12

By Tuesday morning it was all over school.

"Did you hear about Cindy?"

"Cindy who?"

"Bickford. You know. The kid who nearly OD'd over the holidays."

"Yeah, what?"

"She did it good this time."

"Killed herself?"

"Yeah!"

"No kidding! How?"

"Don't know. A friend of mine lives on her block. Says it must have happened last night. Police and ambulances and her mother screaming and her father crying, like that. She saw them carry her out."

"Heavy. Y'know why?"

I heard the news on my way into school, on the high school steps, and stood there in a kind of daze, shivering all over and sweating through every pore in my body. *No, No!* I screamed to myself. *You didn't! You couldn't! It's not true! How dare you!* I must have staggered and tripped because someone was helping me up and asking if I'd hurt myself, if I was all right.

I didn't answer but pulled away and started back down the steps, back down the street to my car at a run.

"Hey, Jenny! You're going the wrong way!" someone yelled.

I clutched the ivory heart at my throat and kept going. *Liar! Liar!* I cried. *You said you'd see me Wednesday!* How could she; she never gave me a chance! I'd phoned last night. Twice. Even knowing she'd said she couldn't see me. Had she heard it? The phone had rung and rung. Had she heard it while . . . Oh, God! Cindy, why?

Driving away I went over all the times I'd spoken with Cindy lately, searching for clues. She'd seemed so normal. Look how she'd pulled herself together. She was working well again, dressing neater. Why now?

And then, suddenly, a little voice reminded me of the gift she'd given me. Automatically, my hand went to my throat. Daddy's warning: "Has she talked about giving away any of her things?" He had warned me. Why hadn't I told someone?

By the time I pulled up in front of the hospital I was crying. I left the car in a wheelchair space and ran into the building. On the surgery floor I asked for my father. The nurse said he'd just finished a surgery and was washing up, but she'd page him. I walked the hall back and forth, back and forth, terribly agitated until he appeared, still wearing his green hospital gown and cap.

"Jen, what's wrong?" he asked immediately.

I flew to him and buried my face in his chest.

He pried me away and led me to a bench down the hall, away from the nursing station. "Now, what is this?" he asked. "What's happened?"

I told him about Cindy, gulping tears as I spoke. Told him about getting the gift and not warning anyone as I should have, as he had told me to, so that I was probably the only person who might have saved her. "But she seemed so much better, Daddy! So normal!"

Dad nodded and took my hand. He didn't say anything for a few seconds, then shook his head. "It's not your fault, honey, so don't go blaming yourself. If anything, it's mine. I didn't tell you enough."

A disembodied voice called, "Dr. Brody, Dr. Eugene Brody," and a doctor came hurrying down the hall. I leaned against Dad's shoulder. He smelled of Old Spice and disinfectant. "What, Dad? What didn't you say?"

He nodded absently at a nurse who greeted him. "Sometimes the suicidal person seems to get better. You think maybe it's because whatever personal agony he was suffering has been resolved. Or maybe he saw professional help. Whatever. But the signs of health return. Sleeps better, doesn't seem depressed, eats better, sees friends again, may even regain something of a sense of humor. But it's an illusion. That's when you have to be most on the alert."

Dad paused and looked down at me. "The calm has come about when he's made the decision. Last week sometime Cindy must have made up her mind to end it all. She set herself a deadline to finish the schoolwork she'd missed, to clear up her affairs, to give away the things she'd not need anymore. She must have thought it out very carefully, and it gave her peace of mind. That's what you observed. You couldn't help being taken in. Even her own parents were."

Was it human nature not to want to see what might be too painful to face, or too difficult to change?

For a moment I saw myself standing at the top of Mammoth Mountain. Wanting out. Now, *I* was alive and Cindy wasn't.

"I devote my whole life to saving life and this child, with everything to live for, squanders it," Dad said softly. "Why?"

I sat up and wiped my eyes. "She felt unloved, Daddy. She felt stupid and ugly and unloved." I looked directly at him. "She hardly ever saw her father." I paused to let that sink in. "Maybe her family was falling apart and life didn't have meaning. Maybe she felt things would never get better. Or they'd be better without her."

Daddy stared at me for a long time without saying a word. Then he looked away. "Come, Jenny. I've got to look in on a patient. Let me walk you to your car. Are you going back to school, or what?"

"Home."

"Will Mother be there?"

"I don't know."

"Will you be all right?"

Boldly, almost insolently, I said, "Yes, Dad. I might have done what Cindy did a few weeks ago, at Mammoth, in fact, but not anymore." It finally had come completely clear to me that I couldn't expect Mom or Dad or Brian or anyone else to be responsible for my happiness. It was all up to me.

Our eyes met. "Mammoth?" Dad asked. Something about his eyes made me believe he suddenly saw the whole vacation as I'd seen it, saw our family for the first time as it seemed to me.

At the car he kissed me and held me close for an instant. "Jenny, you'll be all right. We'll all be. You're not alone. We love you and we do love each other. We *are* a family."

"Are we?" I felt like adding, Prove it. Don't just give me words. But I didn't dare.

Mother wasn't home. Drizzle or no, she was probably out playing tennis. She'd lunch at the club and then go on to her Cuisinart class. I parked in the back, let myself in through the kitchen, and slipped up to my room to the sounds of the vacuum cleaner downstairs. For the rest of the morning until the cleaning service left, I lay on my bed curled up in the fetal position, allowing myself to imagine how Cindy must have felt at the last. If only, I kept on thinking . . . if only I'd asked her to lunch that day, told someone about the gift, gone over there when the phone didn't answer. If only.

I must have fallen asleep because I awoke suddenly to the sound of dogs barking. For a moment I lay in bed, remembering. And then I looked at the digital clock on my bedstand. Two thirty. I sat up quickly and slid into my shoes. At three o'clock I was due at the convalescent home. If I didn't leave immediately, I couldn't make it on time. Solomon and the others would wait a few minutes, but then they'd have to perform without the piano. They were counting on me. If I didn't come, they'd worry. I had to go, no matter how I felt.

I made it to the Shalom Convalescent Hospital in record time, parked in a lot between the hospital and a mortuary, and rushed into the modern one-story building. "Do you know where the Sunshine Seniors are performing?" I asked breathlessly. The nurse at the front desk directed me down two long halls, past rooms containing hospital beds, to a large room which probably served the hospital as a combination dining hall and lounge. The kitchen band members were still setting up. In front of them sat some thirty or so people, some no older than the Sunshine Seniors.

I hurried over to Solomon. "I'm late. Sorry," I whispered.

"Don't apologize, darling. You're here. Is the piano all right over there?"

"Fine." The piano had been rolled to a place just behind the chairs of musicians. My friends greeted me as I squeezed around them to the piano bench. Once seated, I busied myself sorting out the music according to Solomon's program, deliberately forcing back images of Cindy. Then I looked around.

Everyone in our band wore blue-and-white checked shirts and white polyester pants with red-white-and-blue straw hats on their heads. They looked bright, fresh, and cheerful, especially in contrast to the audience.

The audience! Old ladies in wheelchairs, with shawls pulled snugly around their shoulders, stared at us vacant eyed. Spittle ran out of the mouth of an old man seated in front of the band and his head lolled like one of those toy dolls people sometimes keep on the back window shelves of their cars. More than one person seemed to be asleep. Only a few showed any sign that they knew why they were there. What good could come of our performance?

Solomon must have decided that the audience was as big as it would get, because finally he gave us a nod, then turned around. Standing so proudly he appeared to be six inches taller than his five foot four, he introduced himself and our group in a hearty, genuinely happy voice. I couldn't believe it. Didn't he see that he was playing to a graveyard?

But then I became too busy to observe. One by one we played the old favorites, "Peg o' My Heart," "My Darling Clementine," "Man on the Flying Trapeze," and others. Solomon and Becky paired to sing their love song and then Solomon asked the audience to join in singing "When I Grow Too Old to Dream." For the first time, because the music was so familiar, I dared look up. Incredible. Some were singing along with our band. Heads nodded. A few hands kept time. And the old man in the wheelchair, still drooping, spittle still running down his chin, was *tapping a foot*! It seemed a miracle. In that brief time we had stirred something, a spark of life that must have been barely flickering when we came in and was now glowing. I sang, too. Loud and joyfully.

"We'll be back again soon," Solomon promised an old woman as he took both her frail hands in his after the performance. "Good to see you, dear." I wondered if Solomon, or any of the others for that matter, ever saw themselves living like this a few years down the line.

Solomon must have seen something in my eyes because he took my arm and led me aside. "You are wondering, darling. I see it on your face. Is it worth it, growing old? So, I'll tell you. Old age is just like any age, only more so. You got to keep moving. You shouldn't let yourself stagnate. When I was in the hospital last year I was very depressed. My mind got all foggy. So what did I do? I wrote a poem. It gave me something to do and took away the depression. To write a nice poem you got to think, so pretty soon the fog in my head cleared up, too. It's not good, growing old." He gestured around him. "But, it's not bad, either."

He bent to talk with a tiny old lady on a couch. "Hello, beautiful lady. How are you today?"

I ambled over to the refreshment table, pouring myself some punch, and offering a cup to Becky. "We were great!" I exclaimed. "We were really great!" It's the first time I'd thought of myself as part of the group.

"You're surprised?" Hannah hobbled up to us. "You thought we wouldn't be?"

"Now, Hannah," Becky protested. "You always try to start something."

"Of course I try. Why not? If I don't start, there's nothing to finish."

"Always the last word," Becky admonished. She turned to me. "So, tell me, dear. You got a boyfriend? You don't want to spend all your time with old people like us."

"Old people like us?" Solomon interrupted. "Speak for yourself, old lady. Me, I'm not so old. Eighty-six only. A young man yet."

"Hoo, hoo, a regular Rudolph Valentino," Hannah chided. "So, Jenny? Answer Becky. You got a boyfriend?"

"You shouldn't pry, Hannah. It's not your business," Solomon said.

She ignored him. "He's Jewish?"

I shook my head and laughed. They were just terrible, these old people. Pushy, outrageous, manipulative, and embarrassingly forthright. But wonderful, caring, wise, and warm. Survivors. "I know a boy, but he isn't my boyfriend yet. I'm working on it. And yes, he's Jewish." Paul's shy grin came back to me.

"You'll bring him with you sometime, yes? We should see if he's good enough?"

"I'll bring him, sometime," I promised. Maybe Paul and I could play a flute duet together at the center, or I could accompany him on the piano. It was a happy thought. When I got home, I'd phone and ask. And then it was time to go.

As I drove toward home I thought about this very long sad-happy day. Some of the pain and loss had been defused this last hour and now I felt mostly sad and philosophical. The old ones knew the score. Living takes guts. And humor and ingenuity and a lot more. If only Cindy could have known these people, maybe she'd have felt differently. I couldn't imagine Solomon, Hannah, or Grandma giving up without a tremendous struggle. And if they didn't, with all their aches and pains and problems, why should we?

About the Author

GLORIA D. MIKLOWITZ is the author of many books for children. Her most recent books for contemporary teenagers published by Delacorte Press are *Did You Hear What Happened to Andrea?* and *The Love Bombers*. She teaches creative writing at Pasadena City College and lives in La Canada, California, with her husband.